FORTUNE$

Short fiction
by members of
C C WRITERS

The events and characters in each work of fiction in this anthology are imaginary and are not intended to refer to specific places or persons. The work of each author represented in this anthology, whether fiction or nonfiction, belongs solely to that author and does not represent the opinions or thoughts of the publisher, editors, leadership or other members of the Collierville Christian Writers Group.

ABOUT THIS BOOK

These original short stories were written by members of Collierville Christian Writers, based in Collierville, Tennessee. Inspired by the single premise of "FORTUNE$", this diverse collection reflects the creativity and opinion of each writer.

We hope you enjoy this collaboration and that it inspires you to appreciate every moment and find joy in what you have, for true richness can be found in life's simplest pleasures.

Annette Cole Mastron, Editor
Gary Fearon, Creative Director

CONTENTS

PREFACE

We'd always dreamed to attain
    a fortune!
What did we really gain?

We purchased a passenger train —
    a special trip to the moon
We'd always dreamed to attain

Of course there was the pain
    of unknown family and new friends, too soon
What did we really gain?

We financed a new campaign
    to feed all the orphans
We'd always dreamed to attain

We bought an island, outside of Spain
    but now we're secluded, as if marooned
What did we really gain?

Our lives would never be the same
So many options became a boon
We'd always dreamed to attain
What did we really gain?

            John Burgette

AND THE WINNER ISN'T

Larry Fitzgerald

Arthur Williams had resided in the Neshoba neighborhood for thirty years. The retired real estate agent lived in a comfortable, stylish home with his wife, Shirley. A religious man, and an elder emeritus at his church, Arthur was not shy about telling others what he believed.

Eddie Iverson lived next to Arthur. Two driveways separated their houses, so there wasn't much the two didn't see happening between them. No problem. They were friends.

Arthur was the older of the two. Quiet by nature, he enjoyed reading, writing, and nursing an evening wine before dinner. He and Shirley had raised their two boys through college and sent them on their separate ways. Job well done!

Eddie, outgoing and boisterous, was obtuse in the opinion of many. He was single and earned a living running a small machine shop on the brink of bankruptcy. Eddie was not religious and avoided the subject.

One Friday morning, Arthur stood inside a local Super Market purchasing his first-ever lottery ticket. Guided by his three children's birth years, Arthur's lottery number became 19 98 20 01 20 03. Arthur knew the odds of winning the near billion-dollar jackpot were about three hundred million to one, but for two bucks, what the heck!

"What will you do with all that money if you win?" Shirley asked as they sat in the kitchen enjoying the last dregs of their morning coffee.

"Buy a river home for starters," he answered. "Then a big power boat with twin engines, a new home here on lake Neshoba with a meticulously landscaped yard, and two new cars. And, of course, I'll gift some to the church."

"That will be good, dear."

At that moment, Arthur glanced out the large kitchen window. "Oh, oh, here comes Eddie. Wonder what's on his mind today."

Soon, there was a loud bang on the door, followed by the door opening.

"Hey, anybody home?"

"In here, Eddie."

Eddie stepped inside, carrying a box of maple bars.

"Brought you something. You like maple bars, don't you?"

"We love maple bars, thank you. Sit down, have some coffee."

"I can't stay long. Got to go to work today."

"I thought you were the boss."

"That's right. It's payday today, and I'm not sure I will make payroll. Things are tough right now."

"When are you going to give it up, Eddie? Sell the business and move on to something else?"

"Like what? Win the lottery, maybe?"

"Hmm, speaking of that, you're not going to win the lottery tonight, Eddie. I just bought the winning ticket."

"Really? And how many tickets did you buy?"

"One. That's all it takes, you know."

"Shoot! One ticket? I bought a hundred."

"You bought a hundred lottery tickets?"

"Yeah, more or less. I might buy some more. We're talking a billion bucks here, Bro. A billion bucks. If I win, my problems are over. I'll be a fat cat, like you."

"If you win, I'd better see you in church on Sunday, giving thanks."

"Bro, if I win the lottery, I'll not only go to church with you on Sunday, but I'll buy you a new limo and go to church with you every Sunday for a year."

"Is that a promise?"

Eddie stuck his fists deep down into the pockets of his flowery Bermuda shorts, and deeply serious replied, "Of course."

৵

The following day, Arthur was up early. His conversation with Eddie had tempered his enthusiasm somewhat. He knew his chance—even Eddie's—were improbable at three hundred million to one. He flipped on his computer and went online to check the lottery results. Not surprisingly, his numbers did not match the winning ticket.

Bummer!

He closed his computer and sat back in his chair, musing over what *might have been*. His thoughts were rudely interrupted by Eddie again opening the back door.

"Hey, anybody home?" Eddie's voice boomed across the kitchen.

"In the office, Eddie. Come on in."

"Morning," Eddie said as he slumped down in a side chair.

"You look a little rough this morning, Eddie. Are you okay?" Arthur asked.

"Yeah, I'm okay. Didn't sleep too well."

"I'm guessing you won't be going to church with me tomorrow morning."

"Nope, I won't be going to church with you tomorrow. And you can forget about the limo."

"Sorry, neighbor."

"Do you have any idea how many tickets I bought?"

Arthur shook his head. "No idea, Eddie."

"Good. Cause I don't either. I'm sure it was over two hundred. Cost me a small fortune."

"Look, Eddie. Why not give the church a try? Worshipping the Lord can do amazing things for a man. It can change your life."

"Churches are full of hypocrites, my friend. Thanks, but no thanks." With that, Eddie stood and headed for the door.

Arthur quickly chased him with, "Not in my church, man."

"Later," Eddie said as he departed.

Hypocrites in my church? How can you say that? You've never even been inside my church, Bozo!

❧

Wednesday was trash pick-up day. Arthur and Eddie shared the chore of getting the empty trash bins to the curb and back to their storage areas, depending on who was around that day. As Eddie was absent Wednesday, trash cart duty fell on Arthur.

As was often the case, when Arthur went down to retrieve the trash carts, he noticed debris lying in the gutter consisting of a few scraps of paper and a paper cup or two that had not made their way into the garbage truck. Arthur picked these items up and threw them into the empty trash carts. As he returned up the driveway to Eddie's house, he noticed a scrap of paper lying in the street. Arthur wandered over to get it. The litter turned out to be a slightly tattered lottery ticket.

Hmmm. Is God giving me a second chance here?

Arthur shoved the ticket into a pocket and returned the carts to their storage areas.

Back inside, Arthur began to shuffle through papers on his desk until he found the lottery ticket on which he had recorded the winning number. He then laid the two tickets side by side and read the numbers aloud. The winning number was 20 04 20 10 24 68. The number on the ticket he picked up from the street was the same, 20 04 20 10 24 68. Arthur's body began to tremble.

He screamed out, "Shirley, Shirley, come here. Quick!"

Shirley appeared at the door. "What's wrong? Are you okay?"

"Yeah, I'm okay. Here, read these numbers."

Shirley read the two sets of numbers aloud.

"That's it," Arthur said. "That's the winning ticket."

"Where was it?"

"I found it in the middle of the street."

"Whose is it.?

Arthur put his head down and was quiet for several seconds. Then with an unmistakable look of guilt said, "It's ours."

"It can't be."

"Why not? I found it lying in our street. Shall I go around the neighborhood and ask who might have lost the winning ticket to a billion-dollar jackpot?"

"Don't be silly, dear. It's probably Eddie's ticket."

"Maybe. And maybe it blew in from three blocks away. It's a breezy day today. We'll wait awhile and say nothing. See what happens. Besides, you know what Eddie would do with all that money—booze it up, and blow it away—whereas we would tithe it."

Arthur stood and said, "I know God meant for us to have this ticket, and we're keeping it. That's why he put it on our street, in front of our house. It's a lottery ticket. It could have belonged to anybody."

"You could mention it to Eddie."

"Sure, and he would claim it was his, with no proof. You know he would. Shirley, this is our chance of a lifetime. A chance to be rich, to live a life beyond imagination. God is handing it to us on a silver platter."

Shirley looked away and didn't respond.

Arthur finally said, "I can't understand how you don't get this," and left the room.

⁓

The next day Arthur noticed several cars parked next door and people roaming around Eddie's yard and going in and out of his house. He picked up his phone and dialed Eddie's number.

"What's going on, neighbor?" Arthur asked.

"Nothing special. Just doing some extra cleaning."

"Oh, okay."

"I'm cooking up a batch of barbecue for dinner tonight. You want some?"

"A batch of barbecue? So, you're feeding the whole neighborhood?"

Eddie chuckled. "Nope, just you. You're the only neighbor I care about. I'll bring it over."

"Bring enough for yourself, and we'll have a little wine beforehand. Okay?"

"Great! See you about six o'clock."

❧

Two hours later, Arthur, Shirley, and Eddie were visiting over a bottle of Pinot.

Arthur sipped his wine and looked at Eddie. "So, Eddie, how many raffle tickets did you end up with?"

"Maybe two hundred. I'm not sure."

"You're not sure? Didn't you keep track of them?"

"Man, I don't know. I was knocking 'em back that night. Being stupid, you know."

A short awkward silence ensued, which Shirley couldn't handle. She asked, "What would you have done with the money, Eddie?"

Eddie wrapped his hands around his near-empty wine glass and stared at the floor for a few seconds. "Oh, I'd buy stuff. A new car, a boat, a new house, maybe. But I'd give most of it to Children's Urgent Care Foundation."

"Really. Why them?" Arthur asked as he stood and replenished Eddie's wine glass.

Eddie paused and sipped his wine. "Well, that's a long story, I'm afraid."

Arthur hoisted his glass toward Eddie, sat down, and said, "We've got time, as long as you don't let the dinner burn up."

"No problem. It's in the smoker."

Eddie leaned forward in his chair. "I've never told you this, but I fathered a little girl several years ago. Her name was Mandi. She was beautiful, and I loved her as much as any dad could ever love a daughter. I had her for almost six years."

Eddie began to choke up. Arthur and Shirley went suddenly silent.

Finally, Arthur asked, "What happened?"

"Well, one day, my little girl wandered into a neighbor's backyard with an open gate to a swimming pool and fell in and drowned. She was not quite six years old."

"Oh dear," Shirley blurted. "The poor thing."

After another pause, Arthur asked. "How did you manage all

that?"

"Not very well, Bro. I'm still dealing with it."

"I'm sorry, Eddie, really sorry."

"I know you are, man, and I know you mean that. But here's a question for you. Nothing personal, but where was God when this happened? And why did he let Mandi die?"

Arthur gave Eddie a blank stare. He had no answer.

Eddie rose clumsily and said, "I'd better rescue our dinner."

∽

Late that night, Arthur was sitting at his desk when Shirley wandered into his office in her robe and pajamas.

"What are you doing?" She asked.

"I checked Eddie's story. Sure enough, I found an obituary on a little girl, born in 2004 and died and interred in 2010. Her name was Mandi Williams, daughter of Arthur Williams."

"Oh, dear. Did it give the cause of death?"

"No, but get this. Mandi was born in 2004 and died in 2010. Those are the first eight numbers on the winning lottery ticket. Is that a coincidence?"

"You tell me."

"Well, I'd like to make certain before we give away our billion-dollar ticket."

"And how do we do that?"

"Pray…something we should have been doing from the beginning."

∽

The following Saturday, Arthur picked up his Bible and sat in a comfy patio chair with a cup of coffee, ready to spend some quiet time in meditation and prayer. He knew he had two confessions on his list that morning, one for God and one for Eddie.

His confession to God was simple. He turned to John's First

Epistle, Chapter One, Verse Nine, and read aloud, "If we confess our sins, He is faithful and righteous to forgive us our sins and to cleanse us from all unrighteousness." Putting his Bible on the table, Arthur closed his eyes. He confessed to God he had been dishonest with Eddie in not disclosing he had found a lottery ticket that probably belonged to him and had intended to keep it for himself. He asked for forgiveness.

Moments later, as if by divine intervention, Eddie came out of his house and started down the driveway to retrieve his morning newspaper.

"Hey, neighbor," Arthur called out. "Let's talk."

Eddie walked across both driveways and plopped down near Arthur.

"And what is on your mind this morning, Arthur?"

"First of all, I want you to know you were right when you said there were hypocrites in my church."

"What do you mean?"

"I mean, we have a hypocrite in my church. And it is me."

"How's that?"

Arthur pulled the lottery ticket out of his pocket and slid it across the table to Eddie. "I believe this is yours."

Eddie picked up the ticket. His body began to shake. "This is mine! Where did you get it?"

"I found it in the middle of the street."

"I can't believe it," Eddie shouted. "I've been looking for this ticket. I knew I had it somewhere. I just knew it!"

"I'm sorry, Eddie. I should have given it to you earlier. Will you forgive me?

"Of course. You could have kept this for yourself. I would have never known. Thank you for being so honest, man!"

Arthur sat back for a few minutes, allowing Eddie to revel in his newfound fortune.

Then he said, "Eddie, I think I can answer your question of why God took Mandi home so early in life, if you'll allow me."

Eddie's eyes locked up with Arthur's. "Go for it."

"I believe God knew your plans for the dollars you would win from the lottery. He wanted to work through you and Mandi to heal children worldwide. Your generosity will save thousands, maybe millions of children. Mandi will be known the world over, thanks to your gift."

Eddie blinked away a tear. "Thank you, neighbor."

"By the way, Eddie. What do the last four numbers on your ticket stand for?"

Eddie smiled and said, "The 24 68? You'll probably laugh, but Mandi and I used to play a silly little game together."

"What was that?"

"Well, it went like this, I'd shout out, TWO, FOUR, SIX, EIGHT, WHO DO I APPRECIATE? MANDI! Then she'd shout back, TWO, FOUR, SIX, EIGHT, WHO DO I 'PRECIATE? DADDY! YEA!"

Eddie's eyes got bleary. "We played it a lot," he said.

"I love it," Arthur uttered.

"Thanks, neighbor. Now, I have a confession for you."

"Oh? What's that?"

Eddie grinned and said, "I like myself best when I'm with you."

Arthur grinned. "Church starts at 9:30 tomorrow."

Eddie chuckled, "I'll be ready, Bro."

A POUND OF CURE
Barbara Ragsdale

Jerry stared at the bills. *Past Due* blinked like a red neon sign. "You've got six weeks," the banker said. "Pay the bills!"

Whomp, whomp, whomp! Sharp rapping rattled the flimsy apartment door. Jerry gasped before remembering to breathe. He gripped the knob, expecting deputies to bark, "You've been served."

Instead, a stranger loomed there shrouded in white, massive wings splayed out behind him and balled up fists rooted firmly on his hips. Stale air rested in Jerry's lungs.

"Well, let's get this over with," the figure said, pushing Jerry aside to enter the room. "You're in a pickle and I'm busy." As he wheeled around to face Jerry, his wings brushed the ceiling. "What is it you don't understand about *money in-money out?* If you don't have it, you don't spend it. Got it?" Jerry eyed the television and new speakers sprouting from every corner.

"Who are you?" he asked, stalking up to the pompous stranger, glaring at him.

"I'm in the restoration business and you're about to be restored." The figure found a chair, bending feathery wings underneath him. "Anything to drink?" he asked, legs sprawled out in front, arms propped against his chest.

Jerry fumed before answering, "Yeah—water."

"I hoped for something with a little more … oomph." He hauled himself out of the chair and wandered toward the kitchen.

"As you so cleverly reminded me, I don't have the money to buy anything with *oomph*." The steel left Jerry's backbone, and he slouched on the sofa. *I must be running a fever*, he muttered, his hand on his forehead. He focused on the imposing apparition in his apartment. "Are you an angel?"

"Sort of … but not one who waves a wand. A wand-waving

miracle couldn't save you right now." He shuffled over to another chair. "Call me "Use'ta" as in "*I Use'ta do this or that before I ran out of money."* Understand?"

Jerry withered at the reminder. "If you're not going to perform a miracle, then … what are you going to do?" he growled.

"I'm not going to do anything, but you, my foolish little friend, are going to do enough for the both of us. Stop whining and let's get busy. I'm only here for a short while," thumping Jerry in the chest. "I've got a job for you." Jerry's eyes shot up.

"What … and where?" Jerry bolted off the chair.

Use'ta wiggled his fingers. "Not so fast. There's a condition." Jerry's eyebrows bunched together. *Humph! Nothing's ever free.*

"And the condition?" he drawled. "I'm not robbing a bank and I'm not selling drugs, so if that's your solution, I'll just go to jail," he declared, stomping into the kitchen where he filled a coffee mug.

"Don't be silly, boy. I've got a job for you … a real job. The condition is you have to agree to accept it … whatever it is." Use'ta stood ramrod straight, waiting for an answer.

"I must be crazy," Jerry mumbled to himself. "Who would agree to that? No, no. First, where's the job? Oh, forget it. I'm not having this conversation with … what are you really?"

"Nuh-uh," Use'ta answered, shaking his head. "Agree first … then I'll tell you about the job." Jerry plopped on the worn-out sofa. He surrendered to the ridiculous condition. Use'ta sat across from him and bent forward to speak.

"Saint Mary's Soup Kitchen needs a dishwasher."

Jerry jumped up off the chair, shaking his head, pointing his finger.

"No, no, no! I'm not washing dishes for you or anybody. I'm in PR—Public Relations." He marched around the room, his arms in the air, calling upon the saints. "Go away, you figment of my imagination. I don't need your help."

Use'ta waited. "You might want to hear the rest before throwing me out the door."

Jerry turned to face the winged figure. "If you agree to wash dishes for 30 days, all past due accounts will be paid and you will have a deposit of $100,000 in your bank account."

Jerry landed in a dizzying heap on the floor. "Who would do that?" he whispered. "How do I know you'll keep your word?" challenging, mustering up his strength.

Use'ta marched to the door. "Are you questioning my veracity, boy?"

Jerry flashed him a tooth-filled sneer. "No … just your truthfulness." Use'ta studied the lump in the floor. His wings swept the ceiling.

"Visit your bank, ask for Ms. Swanson, and your benefactor is *Anonymous*. Decide how much your pride is worth. Washing dishes or jail." Use'ta pivoted on his toes and swaggered out the door, wings and all.

"You better get your *PR'd* body moving, boy," Use'ta yelled. "They're waiting—the pots and pans, that is," laughing out loud. "Ask for George," Use'ta roared back as he hit the sidewalk and disappeared.

Jerry pinched himself, ran his hands through his hair and rose to look in the mirror. He darted to the door, peering out to see Use'ta—who was long gone.

He grabbed a jacket, flexed his fingers, cracked his knuckles and said, "Bring on the pots and pans." *I can do anything for 30 days. Washing dishes can't be that hard.* Ignorance is ignorance!

Jerry got lost on his way to St. Mary's. The three-block stroll from his parking place to the church let him think about the *Paid in Full* bills … and the $100,000. A smile creased his face.

Brilliant sun roasted the sidewalk. He gawked at the line curved around the block. Well-dressed professionals were sandwiched in between people whose belongings spilled out of shopping carts, waiting for lunch.

He weaved through the crowd, sidestepped carts, nodded to the suits and entered a large hall bustling with activity. Paper-draped tables and folding chairs filled the cavernous space. He approached a bedraggled man barking orders. "Are you George?"

"Yeah … and you are …?" Wrapped in a white apron, George

resembled the dough boy chef. "It's time to serve," he reminded the employees—helpers or… Jerry couldn't decide who the people were. *Maybe they are forced volunteers … like me.*

"I'm Jerry Malcolm … here to wash dishes," he said, ignoring the lump in his throat. He didn't want to be here.

George eyed him cautiously. "I don't know what angel found you because I didn't know until five minutes ago that I needed a dishwasher. Fired the last one—fell off the wagon. A year sober and he decides to celebrate. The kitchen's a disaster. Well, let's get started." George pushed open the swinging doors to the kitchen and Jerry peered around him. He staggered at the massive piles of pans.

George weaved between the cooks who juggled hot food pans. "Hey, everybody! This is Jerry. He's washing dishes. Help him out, please." George draped an apron over Jerry's arm, pointed to gloves and showed him the deep sinks. "Ever done this before?"

"Nope, this is a first," Jerry answered. George smirked, marched down a row of counters, sinks, and began the rapid training session.

"Everything's pre-washed. Scrape off the food. Wash in this sink, rinse in this one, sanitize here and load the dishwasher. Sanitizing wash is ten minutes. The water is hot. You keep going until there's nothing left." With a smile, he twirled around and flew out the door, ready to welcome the dinner guests. "Better roll up the sleeves of that designer shirt before you start," George bellowed.

Jerry flopped down in a chair. *I don't have to do this; I can leave right now—but the bills won't be paid.* Jerry stood, dropped his jacket and rolled up his sleeves. He donned the gloves and grabbed a grimy pot.

"Spaghetti must be the main course today," he muttered, judging by the sauce sticking to the pan. His whole arm and head were inside the pan. He grabbed the spray faucet to rinse, and water flew back in his face. George waltzed in with more pans.

"You gotta watch that sprayer. Water goes everywhere." Jerry glared. George ignored him.

Jerry wiped his face with a paper towel. "Pans too large for the dishwasher, what do I do with them?" he asked, catching George before his furious stride exited the swinging doors.

"They're washed, rinsed and dropped in the sanitizing water. Let them air dry on those shelves." George swooshed out the door. Jerry stretched, his back already screaming from bending over the sinks.

"How long do I work?" he asked the air between the swinging doors. The staff giggled and George whooped.

"Not long … just until it's all done." Lunch over, Jerry scrubbed the last pan, emptied the sinks and wiped down the counters. He stripped off the gloves, massaged his back, and decided he'd crawl out the door. He marked an X on the calendar above the sink. *Twenty-nine more; I'll never make it.*

He searched for George and found him slouched in a corner, eyes closed. "S'cuse me … what time tomorrow?"

George raised one eyelid. "Cooking starts at 6:30; pans soon after," he replied, all his bluster and bravado gone. "Come in around 7:30. Reuben should have all the dishes in the ovens by then."

His jacket thrown over his shoulder and thumb crooked inside the collar, Jerry asked, "By the way, what's your last name?"

George stood and curtsied in a low bow, "I come from a *long* line of Murphys."

"I don't know any Murphys." Jerry waved goodbye. He trudged to his car, every bone in his body hurting. He walked in the apartment, flopped on the bed, and was snoring before his head struck the pillows. His last thought, *the bank* . . .

Within days, Jerry found a routine: dirty, clean, sanitize and dry. Mac and cheese proved a favorite on the menu, but roasting chickens gave the kitchen a mouth-watering scent. He worked alone in the afternoons. Huge pans of cobblers disappeared every day. The cooking staff ignored him, except Reuben, a robust man, six feet and two hundred pounds. "How's it going, Jer?" he'd ask. "Sure 'preciate your work," and walk away with a laugh that filled the room.

Reuben zigzagged through the prep area, giving orders to the cooks. "Needs a little more salt," or "Easy on the pepper." Then he'd smile that huge grin and add, "Let's make a crumble crust for the apple cobbler … sugar, cinnamon and butter. Give the folks some comfort food." Reuben had spent years on the street, climbed out of the bottle and ate at a soup kitchen like this one. Now he served.

Jerry went to the bank; money was there. He only had to last thirty days. Then he met Caleb and Miss Tillie.

Immersed in cruddy pans, he heard a voice behind him. "Hey, mister … could I have more 'zert?" A chubby little fellow, chocolate brown skin and a smile as wide as the space between his front teeth peeped around the swinging doors. His dark eyes flitted while his feet danced in scruffy shoes, sneakers almost a size too small. Jerry guessed his age at nine.

"Are you with your mom and dad?"

He flicked his thumb, "Yeah, they just went outside, but I'm still hungry. You know … just a little more pie," he pleaded, bouncing on the balls of his feet. A gut feeling said this one was a runaway who lived on the street, no parents. Jerry spooned some leftover cobbler in a bowl, heated it and added a dollop of cream.

"What's your name?"

"Caleb," he answered between heaping mouthfuls. Jerry filled a second bowl. Suddenly, George appeared at the door frozen in place. Caleb tried to be invisible; Jerry slid in between the two. George stomped out of the kitchen and motioned for Jerry to follow.

"Who's that?" George snapped.

"Caleb. He said he was hungry," saying as little as possible.

"You can't have children in the kitchen. Where are his parents?"

"Outside, waiting for him." Jerry didn't believe his own words. A streetwise George swept his eyes up and down.

"Finish eating and he's got to go … no children in the kitchen. Got it?"

Jerry nodded, entered the kitchen, and stared at an empty bowl.

Caleb had vanished. *Back to the street unless social services find him.* Sadness filled his soul. Jerry knew about foster homes and living on the street.

⤳

Near the end of his thirty days, Jerry arrived early at the church and realized he was going to miss the soup kitchen. He'd made some friends. Besides Reuben there was Miss Tillie, the warm, sincere woman who drove from her suburban home to sweep her way through the tables, smiling and talking.

She would gently place her hand on emaciated shoulders, and the rheumy eyes of the most hard-core alcoholic would brighten. She'd say, "A little something for you," and stash a gift bag of toiletries beside the plate. She never waited for a thank you. It wasn't gratitude she wanted.

Jerry once asked her, "Miss Tillie, why are you here?"

"I was bored of old business, new business and minutes." A twinkle in her eye, Miss Tillie floated back to the diners.

"Let's get a move on. Customers are waiting," George reminded.

"Where does the soup kitchen get its money, George?" Jerry asked, an idea brewing. "Grant money or fundraising?"

George stopped abruptly. "You ask because . . .?"

Jerry shrugged, "Just curious. Costs money to do this."

"Some people pay for their lunch. Some is grant money, but the majority is from private donations. There's a fundraiser on Friday evening. Wanna help?"

"Sure, what do you need?"

"Dinner and silent auction. Food is catered, but we supply servers; black pants and white shirts. Okay?" Jerry agreed.

At home he curled up for a short nap and woke when he heard a door click. The door was shut, but something was on the floor. A letter and a white feather beside it. *Use'ta.* He'd found feathers before.

Jerry fingered the feather and unfolded the piece of paper. A few words, unsigned. *Good job. I'm watching. Soup kitchen can always use a dish washer.* A sense of fulfillment washed over him, his life at peace for the first time. He had the money, but he still needed a job. Until then, he would wash dishes. Next day he went to St. Mary's, rolled up his designer sleeves and scrubbed pots and pans. George strolled through, patted him on the back.

"Welcome home," he said, sweeping his way around the room, "Time to feed the guests. Wanna serve?" he asked.

"Sure, glad to," stripping off the wet gloves and donning a clean apron. "What's the special today?"

"Mac and cheese. What else?" George shouted before crashing through the swinging doors.

Jerry grinned. *Menu needs work, operation needs fundraising, and I'm home. Find Caleb.*

THE MONEY TREE
Kay DiBianca

"What is that ugly tree doing in our backyard?" Ellen stood in the open patio door, her hands firmly planted on her hips, staring at her husband as he patted the dirt around a tiny sapling.

Tom turned to face her with a big smile on his face. "And good afternoon to you, my love," he said and wiped his hands on the towel that was tucked into his belt.

Ellen stepped out of the door onto the concrete patio and crossed her arms over her chest. "We agreed that I would make all the decisions about decoration, Tom."

"I know, honey, but this little tree isn't really part of decorating the house. Besides, I planted it in the corner by the wall so nobody will really notice it."

Ellen tapped her shoe on the cement. "I don't want it here."

"It's a special tree, Ellen." He gestured to one of the wrought-iron chairs at the patio table. "Have a seat and I'll tell you about it."

Ellen plunked down in the chair and rolled her eyes. "This had better be good."

Tom sat across from her. "I was at the farmer's market today, and I saw an old lady buying groceries. I noticed she paid for the goods with money from a little pouch, but when she turned to leave, I saw her drop the pouch on the ground."

"Don't tell me," Ellen snorted. "Good deed Tom returned the little old lady's pouch of money to her."

Tom ignored the snarky tone. "By the time I caught up with her, she was loading her groceries into a pickup truck. I said, 'Excuse me, ma'am, but you dropped this,' and I handed it back to her." He shook his head. "You should have seen her face, Ellen. It was as if I had given her a million dollars. Then she took this little tree out of the back of the truck and handed it to me."

"A little old lady gave you that tree? And you took it?" Ellen shook her head in disbelief.

"Yes. She called me a righteous person and quoted the proverb that says, 'The root of the righteous will never be moved.' I tell you, Ellen, that lady touched my heart, and she told me the tree would provide a wealth of goodness if I planted it in the right place." Tom reached over and laid his hand on Ellen's arm. "Honey, I know it's not up to your standards of perfection, but it means a lot to me. Let's keep it."

Ellen sighed and looked at her watch. "I don't have time to discuss this now. I have to meet a client in a few minutes to show a house. We'll talk about this when I get back." She stood and marched away.

The next morning dawned warm and sunny, and Tom made breakfast as usual. He took the coffee and food out to the patio and called back into the house, "Breakfast's on!"

Ellen shuffled out of the house in her bathrobe and slippers.

"Good morning, my love!" Tom exclaimed and gave her a peck on the cheek.

"Hmph," she responded and yawned. Then she spotted the little tree. "Oh, no!" she shrieked. "Look at the mess your tree has made!"

On the ground under the tree, a dozen or so ugly brown pods littered the soil.

Ellen rushed over to the tree, drew her leg back, and kicked one of the pods so hard that it ricocheted off the brick wall and broke open. Ellen stood for a few seconds with her eyes as big as dinner plates. Then she dropped to her knees and began breaking open the rest of the pods.

Ten minutes later, Tom and Ellen sat at the patio table counting piles of hundred-dollar bills. They totaled ten thousand dollars.

"It's a money tree!" Ellen cackled. "A real money tree!"

"This money can't be real," Tom said. "It must be some kind of joke."

Ellen grabbed a handful of bills and ran into the house. "We'll find out soon enough," she called back over her shoulder.

Several hours later, Ellen returned from her shopping spree. She spread out the new evening gown and expensive jacket on the bed. "I paid for these with the cash from the tree." She clapped her hands together. "Oh, Tom! We're rich!"

Tom shook his head. "Ten thousand dollars doesn't make us rich."

"It does if it comes from a money tree," Ellen giggled. She picked up the gown and held it in front of her. "This gown cost me seven hundred dollars, and I paid for it with money from our tree. Nobody said a thing." She whirled around the room.

Tom frowned.

Ellen dropped the gown back on the bed. "Let's go see if there're any more pods," she said and rushed to the patio. The little tree still sat in the corner, but there were no more pods.

The next morning, Ellen got up much earlier than usual and ran to the patio. "Tom!" she screamed. "The pods are back!"

Ellen quickly gathered up the new pods, and they counted another ten thousand dollars. She pulled out her cell phone and punched numbers into the calculator. "If we get ten thousand dollars every day for a year ..." She bit her lower lip as she concentrated. "... In one year, we'll have three million, six hundred and fifty thousand dollars!" She jumped up and did a happy dance around the table, shouting, "We're millionaires!"

At ten a.m., Ellen was dressed and heading out the door.

"Are you off to work?" Tom asked.

"Heavens, no. I'm cutting back my hours at the office." And before he could reply, she had stuffed the money in her purse and was gone.

At three o'clock that afternoon, Tom was in his home office, trying to concentrate on his accounting business when the doorbell rang. A muscular man in a blue flannel shirt and jeans stood just outside. "Delivery," he said and handed Tom a paper.

"We didn't order anything," Tom said.

The delivery man pointed to the paper where Ellen's signature was plainly written. "You've got a whole room of furniture here, Mack. Where d'ya want it?"

Ellen drove up. "Oooh. The new furniture!" She breezed into

the house and beckoned the movers to follow her. "In here."

After the new sofa, chairs, large screen TV, and grand piano had been set up in the living room, Ellen directed the movers to put the old furniture in the garage.

"Where are we supposed to park our cars?" Tom asked.

"No prob," she said. "I hired a moving company to haul the old stuff away."

Tom shook his head and muttered something about not counting your pods before they hatch, but Ellen didn't hear. She was too busy adjusting the new throw pillows on the couch.

Ellen was spending money faster than the tree could make it. A few days later, Tom heard the garage door open, a sound he had come to dread. Ellen drove into the garage in a new Mercedes S-class coupe. She jumped out of the driver's seat and spread her arms wide. "What do you think of my new wheels?"

Tom gasped. "Ellen. What are you thinking? That car costs more than a hundred thousand dollars. We can't afford that."

Ellen closed the door and pranced into the house. She patted his cheek as she passed by. "One hundred and eighty-six thousand to be exact, not counting tax."

"But Ellen." Tom followed her down the newly carpeted hall. "We don't have that kind of money, even with the money tree."

She turned on him. "Tom, you're such a bore. I put thirty thousand down and signed a note to pay the rest monthly. It won't be a problem. The money tree will keep dropping pods of money, and I'll keep spending it." She whooshed into their bedroom and called back, "I need to change for my hair appointment, and then I'm going to the marina to look at yachts. Don't expect me home for dinner."

After she left, Tom went to the back door and peered out at the little tree in the corner of the patio. He thought maybe he should pull it up and throw it away. But it was too late. They were already deep in debt and depending on the tree to get them out. Tom shook his head and trudged back to his office.

A few weeks later, Ellen came home from the office with her face flushed and excitement in her voice. Tom braced himself.

"I've done it!" she cried. "The coup de grâce to all my colleagues in real estate."

In a trembling voice, Tom asked, "What have you done?"

"I sold that big, gorgeous mansion up on the hill. You know, the one that everyone drools over, but nobody can afford."

"That's great, honey." Tom breathed a sigh of relief. "I guess that means you'll get a big commission. Who bought it?"

"We did!" Ellen raised her arms in an attitude of victory.

Tom stumbled backward. "You can't mean it. That house was on the market for over a million dollars."

"One million, five hundred thousand. And it's all ours." She grabbed Tom and hugged him. "We've arrived!"

Tom tried to catch his breath. "We can't afford that."

"Of course, we can. I put ten percent down, and I've already signed the papers. We can pay off the mortgage with money from the money tree." She hugged herself and laughed madly. "On top of that, I quit my job so I can spend all my time decorating the new house."

Tom sank into a chair. "Ellen, this has to stop."

"No! Don't you see? It never has to stop." Ellen skipped into the kitchen and poured herself a glass of sherry. "Two weeks from today, we move into our new mansion."

On moving day, Tom packed cardboard boxes with the contents from his office. The movers boxed everything else in the house while Ellen directed them. After all the furniture was out, she arranged for someone from the local nursery to move the little tree.

"That is one ugly tree," the nurseryman said when Ellen pointed out the money tree. "Are you sure you want to take it?"

"It's very special," Ellen said and gently stroked one of the limbs. She watched as he dug around the base of the tree.

"I'll have to trim the roots," he said. "The taproot is too long to dig out."

"Just be careful that you don't damage the tree," she said and stood over him as he worked.

Ellen followed as the nursery worker took the tree to the new house and showed him the spot in the formal gardens next to a brick wall where she wanted it planted. While she watched, the nursery worker dug a large hole, lined it with rich, loamy soil, and lowered the tiny tree into the ground. Then he carefully patted dirt around its base.

"Thank you for your help," Ellen smiled and handed the man a one-hundred-dollar tip.

When Ellen awoke after the first night in her new mansion, she noticed the usual aroma of coffee was missing. When she got to the kitchen, she found Tom looking through the cabinets and refrigerator.

"There's no food here," he grumbled and grabbed his coat. "I'm going to McDonalds."

Ellen was too excited to eat anyway, so she gave him a little finger wave and then ran to the large den, pulled open the French doors, and stepped onto the back porch overlooking the gardens. She walked down the stone steps, feeling like the princess in a fairy tale. When she rounded the corner, she stopped cold.

There were no pods under the tree.

"No!" Ellen screamed and ran to the tree. She searched the ground to see if the pods had blown away, but they weren't there. She fell back onto the dirt path, smudging her new Yves St. Laurent silk bathrobe, and forced herself to breathe deeply. "It's just because we moved," she said. "The tree will start to produce money again as soon as it's accustomed to this new place."

As the months dragged on, the money tree didn't produce a single pod, and Tom and Ellen were forced to declare bankruptcy. The bank repossessed the house and the car dealership took back the Mercedes. They held a garage sale to raise enough money to move into an apartment. The last thing Ellen saw as the new owners moved into the mansion was the little tree being thrown into a trash pile.

In the following year, Tom and Ellen learned to live on his modest income as an accountant. The real estate firm Ellen had worked for refused to hire her back because she had offended so many clients.

At first, Ellen was despondent, but after a few months she

noticed that her life was more peaceful than ever before. She and Tom ate a tranquil breakfast together each morning, and walked in the park, hand in hand, in the afternoon. Tom encouraged her to try her hand at writing, so she joined a local writers' group. Several of her short stories were published in magazines, and she felt a sense of accomplishment she had never known.

One day Ellen stopped at the farmer's market to shop for organic vegetables. As she browsed the aisles, she noticed an elderly couple paying for a bag of onions. When they turned to leave, the husband dropped a wad of paper money on the ground.

Ellen hurriedly picked up the roll of hundred-dollar bills and glanced around. No one was watching her. She could easily slip the cash into her purse. She stood transfixed, thinking of all the nice things she could buy if only she had this money. But then she thought of her life with Tom and what that meant to her. She ran after the couple and called out, "Sir, I think you dropped this."

The man turned and took the money she was holding out. "Gosh darn, Maude," he said to his wife. "Look at this. I'd have lost all this money if it hadn't been for this honest young lady." He smiled at Ellen. "It's mighty decent of you to return it, ma'am. Let me give you something for your trouble." He took a plant out of the back of his truck and tried to hand it to her. "You'll get a lot of good …"

"NO!" Ellen screamed and ran away.

The old man looked puzzled, but his wife just shook her head and sighed. "Dang it all, Ferg, I've told you a hundred times to stop trying to give those plants to every Tom, Dick and Harry you meet. Not everybody likes tomatoes!"

MONEY, MONEY, MONEY!
Nick Nixon

It was a cold and rainy Saturday morning in Chicago. I was there on business for just a few days, and I brought my wife along so she could do some shopping during the days and keep me warm at night. Since it was the weekend, she decided to drag me along as she searched for post-holiday bargains all up and down State Street…and to carry her treasures.

We planned to have dinner that evening at our hotel and attend a performance of *West Side Story* at the Lyric Opera Theatre. If the live performance is as good as the movie I saw back in 1961, I figured I could probably stay awake. I was just hoping the seats were larger and had more leg room than my last experience at a 'fine *old* Chicago theatre' a few years ago.

Somehow, my trick knee survived Debbie's marathon shopping spree and I got to rest it and my back at dinner. We took a cab to the theatre and fortunately, the live performance of *West Side Story* was every bit as good as the original movie. However, I kept looking for Natalie Wood, Richard Beymer, Russ Tamblin, George Chakiris, and Rita Moreno to appear on stage. When I mentioned this to Debbie, she sneered at me, gave me one of *those looks* and reminded me she was only six years old when that movie was released. Then she asked me if movies were in color that far back.

We had brunch at our hotel Sunday morning and took off on an adventure I had been looking forward to for several years. A guided tour of Underground Chicago. There are multiple underground streets, subways and train tracks under much of downtown Chicago. There are even walking tunnels connecting streets, major buildings and even some overhead passageways. No, these do not include the famous L. Part of this is even lower than the bottom of the Chicago River, which runs through the heart of downtown Chicago. Does some of this actually run under the Chicago River?

I never got a clear answer to that.

Our sightseeing vehicle broke down while we were down there. Fortunately it was in a wide intersection where multiple tunnels merge, and they just pulled it over to the side so other cars, trucks and trams could get by. I decided to get off and do some on-foot exploring, but Debbie chose to stay in the warm comfort of the broken-down vehicle and play on her phone while waiting for the repair people to arrive. She and our tour guide told me not to go too far and, "Don't get lost!"

There were signs everywhere and framed photos, maps, construction drawings and even historical facts and stories all over many of the walls. Did I say I got lost? Wellll…I may have taken a turn here and a detour there and…Yeah, I got lost. No problem. I had my phone, and reception down there was excellent.

It was when I stumbled upon some really good stuff about famous Chicago gangsters from the 1920s, '30s and '40s that led me astray. Hmmm, astray may not be a good word to use here. Not astray as in gangster type astray. More like blindly roaming around this particular area while being totally engrossed in all these photos and stories.

As I *was* completely engrossed by all this, I accidently bumped into a barrier that led into another tunnel. By this time, I didn't know what level I was on, and everything had been well lit…so far. So, I wasn't lost. I was just off the beaten path. This barrier was made up of a couple of those concrete sections they use to divert traffic around highway construction, as well as a few sawhorses and some yellow tape you see around crime scenes on TV detective shows.

Since there were no KEEP OUT signs and there were some lights in there, I didn't think I would be trespassing. I walked around the makeshift barrier and did a little exploring. This tunnel looked very old. The floor was not paved. It was made of bricks, and the walls and ceiling were, too. The lights were light bulbs screwed into tubular wire fixtures that hung from a series of very long extension cords. I felt like I was walking through an ancient time warp. There were construction tools and equipment scattered along this tunnel and, every once in a while, there would be a metal door in the wall. None of them opened. They were either locked or rusted shut.

Then I finally came to one that was partially open. Whatever was behind that door was completely in the dark, so I used the trusty flashlight on my phone and in I went. In I went was not totally correct. It was more like in and down I went. There was a hole just beyond that door. Fortunately, it wasn't a deep hole. I was looking up and straight ahead instead of down. When I see someone walking with their head down, I call them nickel pickers…as if they are looking for nickels. I saw that in a movie onetime and I thought it made sense.

Apparently, I was in what was probably a small storage or equipment room. There were various types of panels and equipment on the walls, which were covered in dust and looked ancient. There were also boxes and trash scattered around the room. The hole I had stumbled into was lined with metal and had a metal bottom with a metal plate that had covered it. I obviously had stepped on the edge, causing it to flip, and down it went with me on top.

But there was something under it. I removed the lid and there were two large canvas bags with leather reinforcements on the edges. It took a minute and then it dawned on me. These looked like the bags armored truck guards used to carry money in and out of banks in those old crime noir movies I love to watch.

I flipped one over and opened it up. As Perry White, the editor of The Daily Planet newspaper used to say, "Great Caesar's Ghost!" It was full of money! Money? Man yeah, I can always use a little extra money…even a lot of extra money. Okay…how could I get these two bags outta here? Since this area is undergoing some cleanup and upgrading, there must be some trash bags somewhere around here.

Bingo, I found 'em…big, black trash bags. I selected four of them and headed back to the treasure. I double bagged both of 'em, put on a khaki work jacket and hard hat I found, and headed out of that area. I called Debbie and told her I had taken a wrong turn and got lost but found my way back up to the surface. I told her to take a cab and I would meet her back at the hotel. I quickly hung up before she could begin her customary questioning and hailed my own cab.

I threw the hard hat and coat into a nearby trash can, jumped in the back of the cab with my newfound wealth, and told the driver to take me to the Hyatt Regency Hotel on East Wacker Drive. I got there first so I emptied both bags of cash in a pile right in the middle of our room and waited for Debbie. When she finally arrived and opened the door, she just stood there with her eyes and mouth wide open. I was lying on the king size bed with money over me and the bed.

I shouted, "Close the door?" After she closed it, she just stood there like she was in shock. She finally spoke, "Where did all this come from?"

After I told her about how I literally stumbled over all this loot, she finally spoke again. "Who does it belong to?" Based on the age of these ancient bills, I assume it was all ill-gotten gain that some mobsters stashed away back in the 1920s, '30s or '40s. I surmised that they were probably gunned down in a hail of bullets before they could return and get it.

She gave me one of her "Are you nuts?" looks I am so used to. I thought it was a plausible explanation, based upon the many film noir gangster movies I have seen about that era. I gave her the job of counting the *loot,* and I called my friend, Sandra, who a vice president of one of Memphis' largest banks. I told her what I had found and gave her an approximate total. I was going to e-mail her pictures of some of the bills so she could find out when they were probably printed and if they are still legal tender. She told me they were. She compared that to other people who find money stashed in old attics or hidden in walls. I thanked her for her good advice and the good news and promised her we were going to take her and her husband, Bob, to the Peabody Skyway for dinner and dancing when we get back to Memphis.

I shared the good news with Debbie, and she immediately started telling me what we were going to spend some of this money on…starting with our kids and grandkids. I told her we could deliver all this in my new Lamborghini!

FORTUNE'S DESIGNS
Karen Busler

"Allen, get in here!"

Alicia ground her teeth and narrowed her eyes at the sound of her boss's grating voice. She hated how he used her last name to address her with no "Miss" or "Ms.", making her a cog in a machine. She did not take kindly to being barked at, either, much less by an incompetent higher-up who took credit for her work whenever he could get away with it.

"Be right there," Alicia called out in a sarcastically sweet way. She tamped down her anger and took her time walking into Mr. Plumlee's office, her high heels tapping on the old hardwood.

"Take a seat," he said, not looking up and motioning to the broken down chair in front of his cluttered desk. The mountains of paper threatened to become many avalanches at the slightest provocation. Not a professional look for an architectural firm.

Alicia perched on the chair, not wanting to become part of such a disreputable office. When she was ready to face her boss, she raised her head and looked him straight in the eyes with her best poker face to mask her disgust with him.

"Allen, I've got good news and bad news for you."

Alicia raised her eyebrows and tilted her head, waiting for who knew what.

"The good news is, your big project has been accepted by our client. They're very pleased with the concept, and want to go forward with it."

Alicia couldn't help but let the corners of her mouth turn up into a grin. She'd put her soul into that design and was hoping this would be her way out of this second-rate firm. Her heart soared at the news.

"What's the bad news?" she asked, holding her breath for the worst.

"The client wants *me* to oversee the changes and construction of the building instead of you. It's nothing personal—they just feel that my greater experience will..."

"Are you kidding me?" Alicia sprung from her perch and slammed her hands on Plumlee's desk, causing the expected avalanches. "Seriously, are you kidding me?" she raged, her complexion turning a shade of red and purple that was not healthy.

"Whoa there, Allen. Like I said, don't take this personally..."

"How ELSE am I supposed to take it? It's MY design, NOT yours. And you're taking away any chance of my advancing in this lousy firm—again! I've HAD it with you, you mediocre, money-grubbing, pathetic excuse for an architect, and a man! I QUIT!! And I'm taking my designs with me because I never signed that company ownership form!"

"But, but ... you can't do that," Plumlee spluttered, taken aback with fear and worry lining his face.

"WATCH ME," Alicia hissed as she snatched her blueprints off his desk. She turned on her stylish heel and stormed out of Plumlee's office, stopping only at her desk to throw her architectural drawings, files, and laptop into a box, and left the building. She jumped into her car and didn't stop driving until she got to her favorite overlook where she could think.

"This is more like it." Alicia breathed in the clean country air and spun around with her arms stretched out, embracing the vista from a high ridge overlooking the city. "I'm FREE of that soul-sucking firm!" After her anger subsided somewhat, she pondered what she would do next while enjoying her newfound freedom.

On her way home she stopped at the grocery store. "I've still got to eat," she mused, "and I'll buy a lottery ticket just for the fun of it. Who knows, maybe I'll win and then buy out the firm and fire Plumlee! That'll give him a taste of his own treachery. I've got enough money socked away so I won't have to work for at least six months. I can take my time researching my next move."

∾

"Hey Alicia, want to go to dinner?" Her long time chum from college, Toni, had called to commiserate with her about quitting and Alicia welcomed the distraction from her woes.

"I'd love to! See you at our favorite place in an hour," Alicia gratefully agreed.

∾

"Tell me how it all happened again!" Toni eagerly pushed. "I'm loving the part where Plumlee looked stricken!"

"Well, it wasn't funny when I stormed out of there, but he had it coming. What a royal jerk. I never want to see that despicable slime ball again," Alicia groused. "Besides, if that lottery ticket I just bought wins, that'll be the best revenge of all!"

"Yeah, well, I wouldn't count on that too much, my friend," Toni warned. "But if you did win it, you could put that idiot in your past for good and never think about him again, which you should do anyway, actually."

"That's true," Alicia said, lazily stirring her margarita. "But still, a little revenge would feel mighty good!"

"Maybe for a moment," Toni admonished, "but then you don't know what kind of ripples you'd set in motion with your hateful actions. Don't sink to his level."

"Okay, okay. I'll just forget about the jerk — he's not worth thinking about, and certainly not worth going to jail for! He's out of my life and that's reward enough right there. I've got bigger fish to fry!" Alicia grinned.

"To bigger fried fish!" Toni toasted and they laughed and dreamed of how to spend millions upon countless millions of bucks.

∾

After four months, Alicia was thriving with her own architectural firm, starting with the design she created for her client at the old company. They loved working with her and she with them. She was getting more business than she could handle and was considering hiring another architect and a secretary. The TV blared, interrupting her thoughts.

Why do the news people keep going on and on about that lottery ticket and why doesn't that person come forward already? she wondered. *Boy, if I'd won the lottery, I'd sure claim it!*

Her phone jingled and it was Toni. "Hey kiddo, I had a thought..."

"Uh-oh, treat it kindly, it's in foreign territory!"

"Ha ha. Very funny. But this is important so I'm going to ask you anyway. You know we keep hearing on the news how nobody's claimed that lotto prize from a few months ago?"

"Yeah, it's crazy, isn't it?" Alicia agreed.

"Well, did you ever check your ticket?"

"I'm pretty sure I did."

"Pretty sure? Or did you?" Toni pressed.

"Let me go look—I'll call you back."

Alicia had completely forgotten about the ticket. Having to start her life over after she quit her job consumed every waking moment, but she knew right where it was. Since it had been so long since the drawing and nobody'd claimed it, she actually had a little hope that she might have won it.

Her hands trembled as she opened the box on her dresser and took out the ticket. Then she found the winning numbers on the Lotto website. 2,13,18,29,55, and the lotto number, 10. She sat stunned and checked the numbers a dozen times. She held the winning ticket in her hand!

"Oh my goodness. I'm a multi-millionaire!" The blood drained out of her—she knew this was going to change her life. She put the ticket back in its hiding place and bounced around the room. She knew she had to move quickly because time was running out to claim it. She also knew she had to have good advice on how to claim it and what to do with it. But first she had to call Toni back. She decided not to tell anybody that she'd won, except for Toni, but even she'd have to be sworn to secrecy until she claimed it.

Alicia couldn't sleep that night, but the next morning she was wired and got to work. After a few phone calls and then meetings with advisors who were experienced with investing big money, she finally claimed the almost $900,000,000. She made it a condition she would remain anonymous, which was her option.

The real work had begun with her new position as President, CEO, and CFO of the money in her newly formed *Alicia Allen Foundation*. She loved overseeing the many projects and architects in her expanded company. Over time, her new activities were thrilling and took her all over the world! She was glad she had excellent advisors and employees to keep everything straight— being wealthy was a lot of work.

Toni was a real friend, keeping Alicia on an even keel with this new life. She especially loved that Toni had become part of her organization as one of her trusted VP's.

⁓

"Hi, Ms. Multi-Millionairess," Toni quipped when she called. "Got a spare dime?"

Toni always made Alicia laugh and kept her grounded. "Afraid I'm fresh out of dimes, but will a million bucks do?" she smiled back into the phone. "Want to go for a run with me today?"

"I can't, I've got some contracts to finish up. I work for a slave driver boss lady of millions, you know. But you have a great time ruining your knees," Toni quipped.

"Okay, I will, and I promise I'll run like my grandma!" She loved their banter, as well as having a longtime, real friend through thick and thin.

⁓

Running along the trail in the park always made Alicia feel great. It was her private time to think, pray, and make plans. Even though she wanted to remain anonymous about the lottery win, news still got out and people eventually knew who she was so she had to be careful.

Creating her foundation for the money to do the most good was excellent advice. She'd already used the interest on the investments for many humanitarian projects worldwide, and the principal was still growing! She even funded and designed buildings, schools, and communities in poorer countries with her expert knowledge of architecture. She was gratified at how quickly she was maturing as a woman of means, feeling comfortable and confident in speaking with CEOs of all kinds. The travel and responsibility gave her an expanded, worldly outlook, as well as being much more compassionate to the needy. She loved how she had grown into a sophisticated yet still down-to-earth woman. She considered herself extremely blessed.

She knew that most people who win the lottery go through it in eighteen months, and she swore she wouldn't do that. She didn't need to own the unnecessary trappings of the wealthy; all the doodads in the world wouldn't make her happy. Yes, she was very comfortable, but she was already doing what made her happy—her work, her church, travel, having real friends, making a difference for so many people in the world, and she was profoundly grateful.

Alicia was thinking all these things as she jogged and barely noticed the man sitting on the park bench. She was usually much more aware of her surroundings but she was in her "thinking zone" and didn't pay much attention. As she approached, she did see he'd gotten up and she swerved to avoid him but he tackled her, knocking her to the ground, pinning her down.

"Well, well, well. If it isn't *Miz* Allen, the stuck up employee who thinks she's too good for the likes of me," the man snarled.

Even in her fear, Alicia recognized that raspy voice and screamed, "Plumlee! Get off of me!"

"Oh, so you remember me, peon that I am to you," he growled at her again.

She struggled to push him off, but he was surprisingly strong for a small man.

"Help, HELP!!" she screamed, squirming on the ground, trying to free herself.

"Now look here, Allen, you're going to hear what I have to say.

After you quit, the company fired me, and they actually brought up charges against me! I've spent time in jail because of you and it's payback time." He glared at her with evil eyes and held her down harder, holding her wrists even tighter.

"You're hurting me—let me go!" Alicia cried, praying he wouldn't kill her.

"I'm *not* letting you go. I saw where you won all that money and I'll bet your people will pay millions for you." Plumlee growled again with a sinister sneer as he tied her hands behind her back and stuffed a wad of cloth in her mouth.

"You really are going to pay for ruining my life. You won't be so nasty to me next time, if you have a next time," he hissed as he roughly pulled her up and shoved her down the path to his waiting car.

Alicia knew she had to do anything to keep from being kidnapped. If she could trip him and make him fall, that'd at least buy her a little time, and she might be able to get away to get help.

"AAAAHHHH!" Plumlee hollered as he went down hard on the gravel. Alicia landed on top of him and tried to shove off of him, but he held on to her and pulled her down again.

"Now you've done it," Plumlee snarled again with pure malice. He pulled a knife from his belt and waved it in her face. He touched the knife to her cheek, with a choke hold to keep her still.

Alicia didn't know if she'd fainted or died, but suddenly Plumlee's weight was off her, her mouth cleared, and she felt free. Even better, someone was gently helping her to sit up, supporting her.

"Miss? Are you okay?" A warm, gentle voice was bathing her senses, helping her regain consciousness. She felt dizzy and had difficulty opening her eyes.

"Miss? Talk to me—are you hurt anywhere?" There was that soothing voice again. She wanted to see who owned that voice and her eyes slowly opened.

She tried to speak. "Who are you? What happened?" she squeaked out, putting her hand to her throat.

"I'm Dave, the park ranger. I heard some yelling and got here as fast as I could. I saw this slime ball about to hurt you and kicked him off of you. He didn't put up much of a fight after that." He smirked and pointed to Plumlee knocked out cold on the ground with his hands and ankles tied.

Alicia saw him and made a face. "He tried to kidnap and kill me," she said as she looked into the ranger's kind eyes and went weak again remembering what happened.

"It's over now," that voice said again. I've called the police to come get this dirt bag, and I'm taking you to get checked out."

"Sounds good to me," Alicia said with heartfelt gratitude and slumped into his supporting arms again.

A month later, after Plumlee's trial and conviction, Alicia felt much better about getting out again, but she hired a bodyguard to shadow her. It was the sensible thing to do. After all, she controlled a lot of money and she didn't want to put herself or anyone she loved in danger again.

There was one special friend she'd gotten to know a lot better. Dave made it his priority to be with Alicia as much as he could, working around both their schedules. At first he didn't know about her millions, which made their relationship all the more genuine. They knew they were going to become more than just friends, and that excited both of them.

Toni and Dave both kept Alicia from getting selfish or greedy or lazy. She knew what was important in life and stuck to her goals, even though that huge amount of money kept calling her to a life of hedonism.

In having this wealth, Alicia learned much about herself and how money affects people, and a lot of it isn't pretty. But when her time on earth is done, knowing she used all her talents being a good steward of the fortune she'd received, she has solid hope to hear the words, *Well done, good and faithful servant; you have been faithful over a little, I will set you over much; enter into the joy of your Master.*

LUCKY ME!
Jan Wertz

Every time I went to the Stop 'n' Shop filling station, I'd buy a local lottery ticket as well as one of the big paying tickets. Who wanted to be a Billionaire? Me! That's who! I gave the clerk my Lucky Number scan card and filed the ticket into the back pocket of my purse, in with all the previous tickets I'd bought. That evening, as the Lucky Numbers Lottery winning numbers were read out, my entire world changed!

Now I look back on that innocent time, and wonder what I would do if I could've known all that would happen…

I'd been raised in the local church, knowing it would be as easy for a camel to go through the eye of a needle as for a greedy wealthy person to go to Heaven. I also knew that many of the Biblical people I'd studied, such as King David, had been favored, yet were wealthy. King Solomon had been prized as king for his wisdom and fairness. I was hardly a wise Queen, ruler of her people, but I'd been brought up to know that wealth was power and must be used wisely.

It took me a minute to believe it when my lucky number was posted as the Lucky Numbers winning number! I was now a millionaire! Wahoo!!

Well, almost. It hadn't occurred to me just how much would come right off the top for taxes. Uncle Sam wanted his cut of $250,000, helping himself to almost one quarter of my winnings. Still. $750,000 was still a very nice sum. I put it in its own account at the Cotton Patch Bank.

My next stop was at my Mama's house. She and Daddy had bought a nice little house where they raised me and my brother and sister. We were grown and off on our own now, leaving the two of them in a house which had seen better days. Fixing that was the first thing on my list! I'd seen the fixer-upper shows on TV. So, I decided to do what the celebrities did; I'd send my parents on a three week cruise vacation, hire a decorator and a building contractor, and redo their house to be their special home.

Mother knew all about my winning the lottery before I ever arrived. She really liked the idea of having their old house renovated, *but* she would see to the renovations, thank me very much. No designing stranger was going to come into *her* home and tell her how it would be renovated. No-siree! And I had another thing coming if I thought so. Oops! I knew I was beaten.

Oh, and while we were at it, how about the student loans my brother and sister had? I assured Mother that those, as well as my own loan, had been paid off right after I'd banked my winnings. Mama liked that idea. She smiled a dreamy smile, and said, "A whole million dollars!"

I replied, correcting the total to a whole seven hundred fifty thousand. Mother turned, looking at me critically. "I thought you won the million."

"That was the amount before taxes," I firmly replied.

"Are you sure? That's awful nice of the gov'ment to hep' themselves to your winnin's."

I just agreed that it was. I could see Mama didn't totally believe the government could be so greedy.

Mama wasn't the only person who knew all about my winning luck. Back in my apartment, my phone was ringing. And ringing. And RINGGGIIIING! After answering it once and finding myself talking to someone who knew just how those lucky winnings should be spent to benefit all the…! The next caller had exactly the same idea, but a different project in mind. I unplugged the house phone. My cell phone began giving little dings, each one listed by Caller ID as 'Potential Spam'. I decided my friends would leave messages, others wouldn't. I checked it an hour later, and had over thirty messages waiting. I turned my cell phone off.

I knew from the local news that our Cotton Patch County Hospital was having money troubles. So, back at the bank, I arranged to have a cashier's check for $10,000 sent directly to the hospital. It made me feel good to know I could make a good sized donation to such a wonderful cause.

Two days later, an envelope arrived from the hospital with an official thank you for this month's donation. The letter went on to say I was a Golden Donor. If, however, I could see my way clear to donate $50,000 next time, I would qualify to be Platinum Donor. If I were really generous, and donated $100,000 or more per month, I would become a Diamond Donor and have one of the new hospital rooms named in my honor. The letter was signed by the Hospital Administrator himself. Wow… Now what should I do? $750,000 only goes just so far… A concept I'd never needed before.

The hospital wasn't alone. I'd donated to a Seeing Eye Dog charity. I'd paid a couple hundred dollars apiece to campaigns to save wildlife, the rain forests, to help buy and preserve some wetlands, and wild birds. Then there were the pitiful requests to save abused animals, and more to cure diseases, many of them ones I'd ever heard of. Did people actually get Tutsi-Magutsi's disease? I received Thank You responses from each of the ones I'd sent to telling me just how much better they could do for The Whole World if only I would give a bit more. If I could afford $500, they just knew I could pass along a little more to Help The Planet! Added to those were three or four more requests related each one of the causes I'd donated to. Charities, each touting how deserving their poor people or other animals, plants, ecosystems… Aaaahhh!

Meanwhile, the rest of my extended family had learned I'd paid off my brother's and sister's student loans. Nice. How about my cousins? Or weren't they worth helping? Uncle George's eldest daughter was working towards her PhD in translating the ancient Phoenician language. One auntie's son had just been kicked out of his third university for poor behavior. His mother said they just didn't like him because he was from out of state. The police said it was for getting into beer brawls. I'd known I had several cousins, but now there were some I'd never heard of before. I was amazed to learn just how many people I was related to, all of whom apparently were deserving of monetary recognition for their prodigious scholarship. Or something.

This was about when I realized just how quickly I'd been going through my three quarters of a million dollars! I knew adopting an endangered animal to be just symbolic, but, if everything I'd donated to came to my doorstep at my little second floor apartment, life would quickly become very crowded. I'd have to house the critically endangered Javan rhino along with the pygmy African elephant. Then there was the brink of extinction Ethiopian Lion, one of the few so called 'Biblical lions' left in the world, and the also borderline extinct South African King Cheetah. I don't think those would like each other or get along very well, especially as they'd have to share living in my small guest bedroom. Considering the weight of the elephant, added to that of the rhino, those two would have to stay in my outdoor parking space, as their combined weight would have them going through the floor, and ending up in my downstairs neighbor's living room. He's already a grouch.

The long and short of the problem is, most of my share of my winnings have been spent on my family or given to charities. All of whom or which are True Believers that there must still be more of those million dollars left. My aunties and uncles have convinced themselves and my cousins of just how greedy I am when I obviously won enough to get them all out of debt and my cousins educated. The charities tell me that if I will just donate a bigger sum, I can buy the world out of its troubles.

As for Mother and Dad, they're on their fourth building contractor and want me to pay the lawyers' fees for suing them for not showing up to do the work they'd been contracted and paid to do.

Please contact me if you know of a lottery winner equivalent of a witness protection program. None of either my family or the charities believe the federal government took two hundred fifty thousand dollars off the top for taxes. Help! I'll settle for a trip back in time so I can burn that cursed lottery ticket! Help! HELP!

BABY, YOU'RE A RICH MAN
Gary Fearon

Lincoln Burke's ability to speak four languages after graduating from college left him reasonably prepared for his life goal, to travel the world. By teaching English as a second language in a different foreign country each year or so, he could eventually boast having spent time in every section of Europe and Asia. Since France was the country he most wanted to see—and since French was the language he had become most fluent in—Paris would be his first stop. At least that was the plan.

His college roommate and closest friend, Steve, had already secured both a career and an apartment in South Bend and invited Lincoln to crash with him until he landed a gig. As a lab tech, Steve made enough money to fund their arrangement, and although Lincoln had a couple hundred he had saved, Steve encouraged him to hang onto it to pay for his teaching certification.

"Just send me a postcard from every country you get to," Steve said.

Lincoln studied for his TEFL exam fervently for three weeks while he awaited testing day. When he took breaks from studying, he watched any French movies he could find on streaming video, all of which seemed to star Juliette Binoche.

"Good luck, Link," Steve said as he headed for work on the fateful morning. "Or better yet, how do you say *good luck* in French?"

"*Bonne chance,*" Lincoln replied.

"Then *bonne chance*, Amigo."

Lincoln smiled at Steve's intentional cross-pollination of lingo and replied, "*Merci,* Muchacho."

An hour later, en route to the testing center, Lincoln stopped to put a few gallons of gas in his Fiesta. Confident that he would end the day one step closer to international victory, his optimism was at an all-time high. So much so that he splurged for a lottery ticket. After all, Steve had wished him good luck in French.

Luck was not on his side, however, when he arrived at the testing center. Fire trucks blocked the street and police officers directed traffic away from his destination. Smoke billowed above the commotion, and Lincoln couldn't make out which building was ablaze.

He parked in an alley, as close as he could, hoping the testing center was not involved and that he could walk to it. Indeed, it was an apartment building on fire and the opposite side of the street was allowing foot traffic. At a safe distance beyond the fire trucks stood residents of the building, watching anxiously as firefighters on ladders focused their hoses through broken windows. One older woman, however, stood on the sidewalk in front of the building, yelling and refusing to be led to safety.

"Lá em cima! Lá em cima! Minha irmâ!"

"Please, ma'am," said the fire chief, "you need to go over there."

Overhearing, Lincoln changed direction and raced toward them, shouting, "She says her sister is up there!"

"Up where? Which window?"

Lincoln asked the woman in Portuguese. She pointed to a third-floor window obscured by smoke. They could barely make out the silhouette of a woman inside struggling to get the window open.

"Move that ladder! Over there!" barked the fire chief.

Upon that, Lincoln and the woman were moved back toward the rest of the crowd.

They froze spellbound as he watched a fireman, clinging to his ladder, being rerouted to the corner window. The sound of breaking glass followed and brought a wave of hope, but an unexpected delay after the fireman climbed inside increased their fears.

Next to Lincoln, the trembling older woman looked like she was going to faint. He took her hand and attempted to engage her in reassuring conversation in her native tongue. The woman returned a few words, never taking her eyes off the window. Lincoln kept her hand in his as the fireman reappeared above with a very thin woman in his arms, carefully placing her in the bucket of his ladder. The fireman clambered in with her, and the two were brought down to waiting medics. As Lincoln's woman left his grip and ran to her sister's side, he heard a male voice behind him. "Pardon me, sir."

Expecting a fireman, Lincoln turned to find a TV camera in his face.

"What was that woman saying to you?" asked a reporter.

"She said her sister is an invalid."

"Say, we're about to go live. Can we put you on the air?"

"Um, sure, I guess."

In the ensuing broadcast, Lincoln explained what little he had to say. The reporter focused on a handicapped woman's life being saved by a passerby. The fire chief eventually joined in to say that the blaze was under control.

Oblivious that a TV report was in progress, the relieved Brazilian woman suddenly came up to Lincoln, kissed him on the cheek, and just as quickly returned to her sister, but not before saying, "Obrigada, Bebê!"

This comical surprise was a welcome respite for everyone amidst the worrisome scene. The reporter, amused by Lincoln's stunned reaction, played it up for the camera.

"And a grateful public shows their appreciation. A hero is a hero, in any language."

⤔

The humorous video clip became a staple of the rest of the day's and night's news broadcasts, and particularly caught the attention of The Morning Zoo on WONZ Radio. Seeking local color and anything entertaining, DJs Sam and Samantha invited Lincoln and the Brazilian woman onto their show the following day. With Lincoln as interpreter, the old woman explained that she had come from Brazil to visit her widowed sister, who was currently recovering in the hospital.

The DJs took special pleasure in the woman continuing to refer to Lincoln as "Bebê" and began playfully calling him "Baby" themselves. It didn't hurt that Lincoln did have a baby face. He took the nickname in good humor, thoroughly enjoying his fifteen minutes of fame, particularly when Sam and Samantha marveled at the fact that he spoke multiple languages.

"We can barely speak one," they said.

Lincoln laughed and explained that the fire episode was a perfect example of why he wanted to help people by teaching other languages.

The chemistry between the DJs and Lincoln was so comfortable that they asked him off the air if he'd ever considered being on the radio. He hadn't. They went on to explain that their sidekick newsperson was about to go on vacation for two weeks and they agreed he'd make a great stand-in.

"The pay is lousy but the coffee's tolerable," they added.

Since he had missed his TEFL exam and it would be a month before the next one was held, he gave it some thought. A little income could only help with his travel intentions. So, for the rest of the week, he trained with the departing newsperson, and the following Monday at 6 a.m., Lincoln "Baby" Burke was on the air.

He delivered his first newscast with minimal nervousness and few beginner missteps. Reading headlines from the Associated Press newsfeed was a cakewalk compared to studying Mandarin. And the ensuing on-air interchanges with Sam and Samantha were fun to engage in now that he was an honorary member of the Zoo.

It was toward the end of the show, during the fadeout of Pink Floyd's "Money", that Sam segued into a subject that Lincoln had forgotten all about.

"Pink Floyd on WONZ, and it blows my mind, Samantha. Someone here in Indiana has 220 million and still hasn't claimed it."

"Still? That's crazy!" said Samantha. "If I'd won half that much I'd have a villa in Monte Carlo by now."

"What about you, Baby?" Sam asked Lincoln. "Ever thought about what you'd do if you won the lottery?"

Lincoln managed an answer despite the distraction of suddenly remembering the lottery ticket he had purchased the previous week.

"No question about it," he said. I'd travel the world."

Sam and Samantha carried on with banter about lotteries and gambling. Lincoln struggled to recall what he had done with his ticket.

"Steve, have you seen a lottery ticket anywhere?" were the first words out of Lincoln's mouth when Steve returned from work that evening. He had already searched his car and the pockets of all the clothes he had been wearing when he bought it. After frantically searching every room in the apartment, Steve was his last hope.

"I don't think so. When did you buy it?"

"Last week, the day of the fire."

"The only piece of paper I remember was one you were writing on while you were on the phone that night."

Lincoln suddenly recalled writing down the address of the hotel where the Brazilian woman was staying so he could drive her to the radio station the next day. He remembered that she carried a big brown bag that tipped over at one point and that he helped her retrieve everything that fell out in his car. Could the ticket be in her bag?

Almost a week had passed and it was a longshot, but Lincoln had to know. He drove to the hotel where the woman had been staying after the fire, praying she would still be there.

A tall, lanky young lady answered the door to Room 114. "Yes?" she asked through the door lock.

"Oh. I'm sorry, I'm looking for a Mrs. Braga. She was staying in this room."

"Just a moment," she said, closing the door.

Moments passed while he pondered the girl's Brazilian accent as well as her very tanned skin, the embodiment of the Girl from Ipanema. He almost lost sight of why he was there when Mrs Braga opened the door wide.

"Bebê!" she exclaimed, throwing her arms around Lincoln and kissing him on the cheek again. He laughed, slightly embarrassed, as the old woman explained to the girl in Portuguese that he was the young man who had been such a hero. From her passionate retelling, one would think he himself had climbed up the ladder to save her sister.

"My grandmother has talked about you all week," said the young lady, extending her hand. "I'm Antonia."

"Hi, I'm Lincoln. But," he added, nodding toward Mrs Braga, "my friends seem to call me Baby."

"She calls everybody Baby," Antonia said with a smile.

Lincoln asked Mrs Braga how her sister was doing. They led him into a room where the older lady sat in a wheelchair, watching TV. Mrs Braga excitedly introduced them to each other, and had she been capable, the old lady would have leaped from her chair and kissed him as well.

He visited with them in their hotel suite for two hours, enjoying their company, honing his Brazilian Portuguese, and especially getting to know the tall and tan and young and lovely Antonia. He learned that she had come from Brazil to serve as interpreter while her grandmother and the sister navigate insurance and other complexities in the aftermath of the fire. As the daughter of a prominent coffee exporter, she had some experience in business affairs.

They appreciated Lincoln's coming by so much that he felt ashamed to reveal the real reason why he had shown up at their door. He was relieved when Mrs Braga suddenly remembered finding something that might belong to him. His heart raced as she left the room to retrieve her bag and then returned with…a parking ticket. One had been put on his windshield for illegal parking the day of the fire and he had left it on the seat of his car.

Lincoln reminded himself that there was still a chance the lottery ticket was *somewhere*. That encouraging thought emboldened him enough to ask Antonia if she'd like to go out to dinner sometime. Receiving a surprisingly demure Yes to his invitation, he thanked them all for a lovely evening and bid them *boa noite*.

"You sounded great on the radio this morning," said Steve back at the apartment.

Lincoln was almost too absorbed in his laptop to notice.

"What? Oh, thanks," he finally said.

"What are you working on?" asked Steve.

"I'm trying to find that girl I met tonight. There are a dozen Antonia Costas on Facebook, and none of them are her."

"Have you tried googling her?"

"I just did, and there are tons more hits."

"Try narrowing your search. Add something specific to her."

Coffee, remembered Lincoln. He typed in *Antonia Castro coffee.*

"Ah, there she is," he said, gazing at a Glamour Shots-worthy photo of Antonia in a business suit on the website of Castro Café Trading. She looked even better with makeup.

"Holy cow. She's the vice president of her father's company. They're Brazil's biggest coffee exporter!"

Steve came over to look. "Holy cow," he echoed. "I see what you were talking about. I wouldn't let her get away!"

"I don't intend to. I'm calling her right after work tomorrow."

The ensuing month leading up to the next TEFL exam saw Lincoln in a routine he had never imagined. Mornings on the radio with Sam and Samantha were followed by lunches with his honorary Brazilian family and evenings with Antonia. She helped him study for his certification, being somewhat conversant in the Romance languages herself. And when they weren't studying, Lincoln made every effort to converse in romance.

When he took her on a tour of Notre Dame University, he anticipated a day when they would see the real Notre Dame in Paris. And the colorful River Lights Plaza in South Bend would pale compared to Rome's Trevi Fountain. It would be a dream come true to have someone like Antonia to share it all with.

Lincoln was so filled with optimism that Steve delayed telling him that he finally found the lottery ticket behind the couch. It was not a winner. Better to let him pass his exam before distracting him with unlucky news.

Antonia, meanwhile, put off telling Lincoln that she and her family would be moving back to Brazil in two weeks. She was even less eager to reveal to him that she was married.

≼

Over the next five years, Steve received postcards from such places as Tuscany, Munich and Tokyo, as Lincoln had promised. At year six, he received a box from France along with this letter.

Hey Buddy,

Samantha and I recently got back from Mrs Braga's funeral in Brazil. It was wonderful to visit with Antonia and her husband once again, even under the circumstances. As always, Antonia's dad offered me a job doing international stuff, but I declined since Samantha loves it here and we're going to make it our home base.

The enclosed is part one of my gift to you. I had no idea Mrs Braga was incredibly wealthy, much less that she included me in her will, and that's part two. When you check your account next week you'll see two million dollars, one for each year you let me stay with you. You helped me out when I only had dreams of being here, and now that I am, I'll never forget it. First chance you get, please come see me and Samantha in Monte Carlo.

Thank you for everything, Amigo. Enjoy the coffee.

GETTING THE GREEN
Judy Creekmore

I've always enjoyed the thrill of unfolding the green and passing it to the clerk along with my marked sheet—even if there's not much chance for the big payout. I watch the TV hoping to see a shot of some lucky working stiff. It's all over the news when there's a winner. For instance, ask a guy on the street and he'll know if someone won the Giganto Lotto for more than $1 billion last month. He'll know the winner hasn't come forward yet. I'm letting *you* in on a little secret—that winner would be me.

Yeah, shocked me, too. Bought the ticket right here at Come and Git It. In the past couple of years it's grown into a routine. On slow days I like to spin yarns with Trey, the young clerk who now runs this place since his dad was killed during a robbery a couple of years ago. I'll be glad when he can sell pickled boiled eggs again from that big jar on the counter. Individually wrapped plain boiled eggs don't go as well with Old Bullet Light Beer. Covid rules messed up a lot of stuff.

Sometimes a buddy'll be in the store at the same time as me. I like when I run into Shorty O'Donnell. I'm average height and he's a good foot shorter. That makes it easier to playfully slap at his jaws if he doesn't see me coming. He'll pretend to be mad—he overdid it once when he was wearing steel-toed work boots and managed to kick my shin. I limped and had a bruise for a week. When I saw him next I could tell Shorty was too ashamed to apologize, so I followed him around the store telling him I don't bear a grudge. I'd tug his hair or pull his shirttail out of his pants to show I didn't have any hard feelings. He couldn't stay long that day and in his rush forgot to buy a lottery ticket. That could have been his week.

Trey's mamma, Coraline, owns the store and since the robbery, she's always there for the Friday night shift. She doesn't want Trey getting in the way of a bullet like his old man did—though she did get a big insurance settlement. Bought a house in the 'burbs and took a four-day cruise to Bermuda, but still…Between 5:30 and 8:30 p.m. is when most people show up to buy the tickets and she knows the cash box will be full because they also get their beer, jerky and toilet paper the same as always. Before the robbery the cashier'd get busy, let the money build up because there'd be only one person working and they couldn't leave the counter. Now, every 30 minutes or so Coraline pulls money from the till and takes it to the office. She puts it in a safe built into the wall. I know this because after the robbery two years ago Trey said the cops told him that store security needs to be better.

Like I said, it's busy on a Friday night. Sometimes I buy a small cup of their Red N Spicy Slush and stand in this corner by the milk and egg section to drink it and watch the people. Not much traffic here except sometimes a mamma needs a gallon of milk on her way home from work. See, the milk's near the frozen drink machine and I can refill my cup without being hassled by Trey or Coraline to hand over my walking around money.

So, I've gotta good view and one night I see Philly Squint come through. He gets a beer and a pack of gum and gets in behind a mamma with a cute kid that's trying to get Philly's attention. But Philly's busy. See, he's checking out the store—the big wide-view convex mirrors in all the corners, and the security door with the bulletproof window that locks when Coraline goes through either way. He notices where she keeps the key at the waistband on a cord attached to a belt. What he should be looking for is the Glock 17 Trey wears in an inside waistband holster. I gave a heads-up to Coraline. I like to watch her in those stretchy pants and top that shows off one shoulder when she bends down to pick a pack of gum off the floor that some slob dropped. She hasn't changed much since high school.

When he's not busy cashiering or stocking or cleaning the store, Trey will tell me to fix him a large coffee with three sugars and make one for myself. He asks if I don't have someplace else to go? I do. I gotta lotta places to go, but nowhere else I want to be for a few hours a couple of days each week. You and me can come together on Tuesdays now that we're both men of leisure.

Let's face it, being a minion at the Port Authority was a pretty boring job unless there was a fire or something. I got outta there as soon as I was confirmed the winner. Told the boss Ma needs me around the house, so I'm taking early retirement. Life is better already. I like being where the people are and they go to convenience stores. If they have money, they're happy. If they don't, you watch them and wonder "What's their story?" Sometimes when I'm feeling flush I'll throw a $5 bill on the ground and say, "Excuse me, I think you dropped this." Sometimes I have to push it into their hands, but mostly they're grateful and they buy a hot dog or sandwich they might not have been able to afford. Sometimes they buy a lottery ticket. Wouldn't it be a hoot if somebody hit it big on a ticket I gave them money for?

See this guy coming in? The one that looks like he's never had a bath and you don't want to stand downwind of him. Name's Sean, but we call him Greasy. Twenty-three years old and he designed a video game. A game! And he sold it for enough to never have to work again even if he burns a bagful of the green every day. Looks sad, right? He's got nothing to look forward to. Maybe he'll design a dozen more games and get more of the green? That's the trouble of being lucky when you're young.

Greasy has this big apartment in Manhattan, but he still comes here to see his old man. It must be nice to live in an apartment in the city. I've always lived with Ma except for a year when I was married, and five years in the Army and Walter Reed Hospital during the Gulf War. Not so lucky those years 'cause that's when I met my ex. She was visiting her brother in the bed next to mine. Enough of her. Ma's family has owned the same Victorian Brownstone for seven generations. It needs work bad, so that's the first thing I'll do when I get the green. She don't know I won yet. I tell her when I win the lottery I'll build her a new house in the 'burbs, but her heart is two blocks over where she puts different artificial flowers in a planter on the stoop every season. Sometimes little girls on their way to school will add a flower of their own. "Get out your phone. Take a picture of the sweet little Carnation that Sophia Wong added," she'll tell me. Look, I gotta million shots of fake flowers in here!

All things considered, I've gotta good life. Can you imagine me with $1 billion? Me either. So, I don't think I'm gonna tell. The financial advisor says I should start a foundation. They'd take care of the money—invest it and hand it out, and no one would ever have to know who it came from. I like that. I'd still want plenty of the green for walking around and instead of dropping $5 on somebody that needs it I'd make it $20. Don't want to get too flashy, have people suspecting I won the lottery, or following me into an alley to see how much I got in my pockets.

Look at the time! You're a good listener, but it's almost time for your mamma to pick you up, big guy. She won't be staying late at the office when the Authority's big project is over in a few weeks, and I'm gonna miss your company. When I get the green she's gonna win a sweepstakes she doesn't remember entering. Maybe she'll go to art school like she told me once before you were even thought of. Trey over there will be offered a full scholarship at Steven's Institute. Whoa, buddy, that's a great smile you got, but you're drooling all over the place like that's a big deal. It's the least I can do since I accidentally shot his old man.

UNEXPECTED FORTUNE
Steve Bradshaw

I grew up in the Texas panhandle, 25,000 square miles of dirt and tumbleweeds and home for less than 2% of the state's population. Uncle Jack traveled the world and made his home in Saint Pierre, Newfoundland, a self-governing French territory on the northwestern Atlantic Ocean 3,600 miles away. Other than my father's stories about his younger brother, who marched to a different tune, I never knew Jack White. That is why I was shocked when he died and named me beneficiary to a bona fide fortune— Captain Kidd's buried treasure map!

Jack traveled the world in search of adventure. One day he found the one that would change everything. He had enjoyed a successful week of gambling in the Bahamas—he turned $1,000 into $25,000 at the casino poker tables. The quiet, well-dressed man in dark sunglasses always puffing on a Cuban cigar lost all his chips. He dropped a dogeared envelope onto the table with a bold challenge. He said it would cost $25,000 to get a shot at winning it in one game of five-card stud, all cards played face up.

In bold sweeping strokes, *Captain William Kidd*—the infamous pirate of legend—was scrawled across the envelope. It exuded the raw confidence of a real pirate. Beneath the faded ink signature was a date—April 7, 1696—written by the same hand.

In the awkward silence, players were reluctant to bite. Then the man's cigar wagged as he described the treasure map inside. He said it was an indisputable fact Captain Kidd buried booty on the east coast in the 1600s. Some of his treasures of gold and silver coins, ivory, precious gems and opium have been recovered, inventoried, and forfeited to the British Crown. The legend of Captain Kidd lives on because some of his treasures have not been found. He used them as a negotiating tool in his trial for murder and piracy.

His efforts failed. He was hung in 1701. The treasure map inside this envelope signed by Captain Kidd is proof enough one of his priceless fortunes is still out there.

The man's story was not why Jack slid in all his chips. Jack had inspected the envelope and the brittle, burgundy-wax seal on its flap. He saw the pristine, detailed impression of a skull and crossbones that had not been damaged—it confirmed authenticity. Jack believed the man with the Cuban cigar was certain of the contents. His fear of a pirate's curse was greater than his curiosity and greed.

When the last card dropped, Jack had a royal straight flush—odds five million to one! Gasps rolled through the casino and eyes locked onto Jack as he raked his winnings into his pockets, cashed out, and started to leave the gambling hall. He stopped at the door and turned to the man with the Cuban cigar in the room of mannequins. He no longer puffed on his cigar. Jack would not understand his peculiar smile for many years for it was not the smile of a man trying to cope with the loss of a fortune. It was the smile of a man who just got his life back!

That night Jack returned to his hotel room and jumped off his third-floor balcony onto a giant palm tree. He slid to the ground and moved in the shadows in fear of his life. He reached a small harbor a mile away and slipped onto a banana boat as it pulled from the pier.

When the boat landed in Tampa, Jack paid the captain for the ride and his silence. Jack hopped a slow-moving freight train that night and got off in Chicago. From there he would hitchhike to Montreal, purchase a used motorcycle, and take his time returning to Saint Pierre. When he got home he hired armed protection and lived the life of a hermit. Jack's days of adventure had come to an abrupt end.

When my father passed, the *Uncle Jack stories* stopped. It would be twenty years later when I received a registered letter at my home in Dumas. I did not know then my life was about to change. I would step into the darkness that comes with a pirate's treasure map.

❧

I made sure everyone in earshot heard me. I leaned on the cluttered store counter and told the world my plan—I would spend a few days and nights on the water south of Martha's Vineyard fishing for Striped Bass. I need not be disturbed. I must have my alone time.

The white-bearded old salt at *Pete's Boat & Fishing Gear Rentals & Bait Shop* rolled his eyes as he slid over the documents for my signature. He did not care about my need to yell and turn heads in his store. All he wanted were forms signed, payment in advance, and I had to buy the boat insurance. When I added a pile of premium fishing gear and two days of the most expensive live bait, Ol' Pete's pipe started to spin between puffs and new totals on his calculator. In the end, he even threw in a used marine VHF two-way radio for free. At the time, I did not know how important that would be.

Prior to Martha's Vineyard, I thought I had done a pretty good job setting up my fake fishing trip from Rochester, New York. How else was I going to get to my secret place and find my pirate treasure? A fishing trip, truth be known I had never put a worm on a hook, and I had only seen the Atlantic Ocean outside my airplane window, once. Texas panhandle life does not expose one to a lot of boats or large bodies of water. Piloting one on open ocean waters at night was something I had not really thought through—but the show must go on and eyes were on me.

Standing on Pete's dock, eyeballing my sixteen-foot Alumacraft rental with the 40 HP Tiller Parsun's outboard motor, I got queasy. Then chills ran up my spine. A sharp pain in my back felt like I had been stabbed with a dull knife. I winced, doubled over, and spun around to the undulating crowd on the wharf. My killer or killers were there! They followed me from the reading of the will in Rochester. I felt my uncle's paranoia—the pirate's curse.

I guess I need to go back a little, the week before Martha's Vineyard. They said Uncle Jack committed suicide. I really don't know about that. I thought law and order had reached

Newfoundland, but I was wrong. I'm no detective but I do not think one pours oneself a scotch on the rocks, ransacks their house, and then puts a gun to their head. Regardless, Uncle Jack's death triggered everything including my Martha's Vineyard mission.

I received the certified letter, very expensive stationery. It notified me of Uncle Jack's terrible death. The letter came from Jack's high-priced estate attorneys, one of the top law firms based in Chicago with offices in Rochester, New York. The very legal letter formally requested I attend the reading of Jack White's last will and testament. I was named as a beneficiary. The reading would take place at the Del Monte Lodge Renaissance Hotel in downtown Rochester in a few days. Inside my envelope was a first class, round trip ticket and hotel room reservation, one night. The small print at the bottom was clear. It said failure to attend would result in forfeiture of all rights to assets. Unclaimed assets would be donated to charities in Saint Pierre.

Behind my ticket was a small, sealed envelope addressed to me from Jack! His note said it is vital I attend the reading of his will because he was leaving me twenty-seven 1934 (G-Chicago) $500.00 FRN VF bills, and each bill was worth $1,795 to collectors. I did the quick math—$50,000! Jack said in addition he is leaving me something no one else would know about. He said his brother could never talk to him without mentioning me. Jack wanted to do something special for his brother and for me. Jack said he wrote this letter many years ago. It was part of a bigger plan launched on the day he contracted with his very expensive law firm.

Jack instructed his lawyers to hold my sealed, confidential letter in a secured vault at their Chicago offices. My letter was to be delivered upon Jack's death. It was clear he wanted me to have his most prized possession—Captain Kidd's lost treasure map. The Kidd envelope holding the treasure map was in a safe-deposit box at the Chase Bank on 1755 Monroe Avenue in Rochester, New York. The key to the box was taped to my confidential letter.

He instructed me to follow directions exactly. I was to say nothing about the Captain Kidd envelope or map or topic. After the reading of the will and distribution of assets, I was to return to my hotel room, alone. I was to examine each of the twenty-seven $500.00 bills left to me. I would find one bill has a circle around the letter "F" in the word "Five" on the lower left quadrant of the bill. The first five serial numbers of the bill is the number of the safe-deposit box in Rochester that my key fits. Inside that box I will find Captain Kidd's envelope with the map. I will also find a deed of ownership made out in my name and registered with the state of Massachusetts. This legal and surveyed parcel of land was purchased from the United States Government and is located on an uninhabited island three miles south of Martha's Vineyard— Nomans Island. Captain Kidd's lost treasure chest is buried somewhere on my parcel of land. Jack wanted to eliminate all questions of ownership for all things found on that parcel of land on a government-owned island.

After I got the nerve to board my rental boat, I left Pete's dock, pains and all. I managed to navigate three miles south of Martha's Vineyard without event. There it was—Nomans Island. Six-hundred acres of empty beaches, wild scrub, and scraggly trees. Ownership of the island had bounced around until World War II. From 1943 on it was used by the United States Navy for bombing practice. In 1996 they gave it to Fish and Wildlife Services. The risk of unexploded bombs and lack of resources led to the island's formal designation as a wildlife habitat closed to the public. Uncle Jack pulled a lot of strings to secure private ownership of a small piece of it. His cover story was he needed a quiet place to write his memoirs.

I landed on the south side and tied the boat to a large, odd-looking shrub. The place seemed dormant. I walked the beach reading my map and looking for landmarks. Location of my parcel was hard because everything looked alike. Then, the very moment I arrived, a massive wave tried to knock me over. When it returned to the Atlantic, a pirate's knife was at my feet.

The gnarled wooden handle stuck out of the wet sand like it had dropped out of the sky. The setting sun lit up the golden skull and crossbones on the butt of the fat handle and two large gemstone eyes seemed to stare. Stunned and exhausted, I opened Captain

Kidd's map to confirm my location on the very unattractive Island. I was able to confirm I was indeed standing on my parcel. The pirate's treasure must be close. Maybe the knife slipped out. What are the odds the Atlantic Ocean spits out a four-hundred-year-old pirate's knife the moment I arrive?

With my nose still in the map, a second powerful wave climbed the beach with such force it knocked me over. I struggled to keep the map dry as I found my footing and the giant wave returned to the ocean. To my surprise the knife had gone with it! How could I let that happen? Any normal person would have grabbed it from the jaws of the sea immediately.

Maybe it was close. Maybe it was too heavy to tumble too far. In desperation I moved deeper and scanned the area as daylight waned. That is when I saw my rental boat; it was bobbing in the water fifty yards out. I remembered I had secured it to a large, odd-looking shrub in a shallow cove. Maybe it was low tide. Then the odd-looking shrub popped out of the water, alongside my boat that was fully insured.

As I sat on the beach, my greatest fears moved from someone trying to kill me to dying a horrible death on a disgusting little island named Nomans. I cannot swim, I'm a picky eater, and no one would be looking for me for at least three days, thanks to my little store announcement.

Another wave dared to climb the beach. This one stopped at my feet. In my depressed state, I was not excited to see the knife returned. Certain I would die from hunger and thirst, I grabbed it and moved to dry land—I might need to take my life. If I had known from the start I would only find a pathetic pirate's knife, I would not have worried about being killed.

I spent the next few days searching for drinkable water and digging holes all over my coveted parcel of land. No one ever talks about the fact that a pirate's "X" is nonspecific. Captain Kidd's buried treasure could be anywhere on my disgusting acre of sand and scrub, and there's nothing on his map about how deep to dig.

I returned to Dumas with the worst sunburn ever and twenty pounds lighter. It took them ten days to find me. I probably would have died on that God-awful island if my two-way radio had not worked at least one day. I had it long enough to get a message onto Pete's radio. They knew I was out here but did not know where to look. Then, Ol' Pete spotted my boat. They stepped up efforts. It seems, like a lost horse heads back to the barn, my rental boat returned to Pete's wharf. Thank God he recognized the enormous, odd-looking shrub in tow—Nomans Island. Pete sent the Coast Guard.

Captain Kidd's treasure is still out there somewhere, on my small parcel of land. One day I will return and dig some more. For now I am happy the pirate's knife had some value. The authentic 400-year-old knife had a large uncut sapphire and ruby, and there was an enormous uncut diamond inside the gold skull and crossbones. It went for $250,000 at auction! I think Uncle Jack and my father would be proud that the money opened a ranch in Dumas for troubled teens. We named it *Uncle Jack's & Captain Kidd's Adventure Ranch*.

$325 MILLION AND THE GOLDEN RULE
Doyne Phillips

"Do unto others as you would have them do unto you" is what we were taught as children, but as we grew older we realized there was in certain situations a more appropriate quote. "The person with the gold makes the rules". I do believe the original quote should be our foundation, but in the real world of business and finance, the latter should be a constant reminder of who is in charge. As a friendly car salesman intent on upgrading my model of choice once said, "It's only money.". I quickly replied, "But it is my money."

My friend Lindel was a lottery winner. Watching the Lotto winners on TV, we had always said what we would do with our winnings. I never expected to win nor for my friend Lindel to win. But he did. We both had discussed what we would do with the money, not realizing that one day one of us would be a winner and would have to put our money where our mouth was. 325 million dollars was the after-tax amount he received. I wanted to see how close Lindel would stick to his imaginary plans. I must say, I love to hear it is after taxes. That seems to imply you have the freedom to spend the remainder as you would like. The truth is, you do, but you must realize the fight to preserve the remainder is now on.

During Lindel's days working in the financial field, he presented a young widow a large amount of money from her deceased husband's life policy. Prior to his death, Lindel shared with her and her husband a statistic that many find shocking. A large percentage of people coming into such money, no matter the amount, have spent it all in eighteen months. The husband decided and she agreed to take those death benefits and put them where they will grow and pay her a monthly amount for life. That was a common practice, easily done, but many times if not stipulated in the payout, the beneficiary—once the money is in their hot little hand—will not follow through. In this case, the widow did follow through with her husband's wishes.

She came in, wrote a check for 85% of the full amount for the lifetime annuity with monthly payments, and kept the remaining 15% for her medical bills and the promise she had made her husband to take the family to Disney World. In order to cover the check for the annuity, she would have to deposit the death benefit in her bank account.

Knowing what she would be going through at the bank, Lindel gave her this warning: "When the bank teller sees the amount of the check you are depositing, they will take it to the VP or President. They will then attempt to talk you into leaving the money in their bank, invested in their products for their benefit. They will explain to you this annuity is a bad idea; they have something better and it will be right here in your hometown. You must tell them you have written a check for the annuity and must deposit the death benefit amount to cover the check, pay your medical bills and do the bidding of your husband for your family. Stay firm in your decision which honors your husband's wishes for you and your family." She quickly responded, "I don't think I'll have this problem because I know everyone in the bank and have since childhood; they are my friends." And off she went to her bank.

Two hours later, Lindel heard the front doorbell of his office sound, and in walked the widow. He invited her back to his office where she began to tell him of her bank visit. She began with, "I thought the people at the bank were my friends! They did exactly what you said they would do. The teller took my check to the officer in the bank. Then they took me to his office. He began to tell me what I didn't want to do and what I should do with the money, which was to put it into their investments. They kept me there for over an hour until I finally told them I had written all the checks for the entire amount of the deposit; it was all gone. How did you know they would do that?"

Lindel again explained the need for deposits and investments in a smaller bank such as hers. Also, many times a bank employee or employees just need your money to meet their goals or bonus requirements. As for the tellers in the bank, many do not know what a lot of money is. Lindel shared with her an interview he once had with a bank teller regarding a job. The teller brought up something about a lot of money. Curious, and knowing he worked with money, Lindel asked him what he considered to be a lot of money? He answered, "Well, I'm talking about something like $350.00." With all that said, let's get back to Lindel's $325 Million.

We are told once we win the Lotto, we need to get an attorney and a CPA. Since Lindel had both, he was ahead of the game. He also had a trust set up, so he would ask his attorney and CPA about depositing the winnings into the trust account. In most cases a trust is protected from everything but taxes. In this case taxes were taken out and monies can only be removed with the consent of the trustees. Fortunately, Lindel and his wife were the trustees, so no problem there. Once done, he turned to spending this beautiful amount of money, doing so with the advice of his attorney and CPA.

In all our fantasy planning, Lindel had always said he would give 10% or more to charity according to his CPA's direction. There are various ones he favored such as The Cancer Society, several Children's Hospitals, and a couple of colleges. He would also set up and fund a foundation in his name, his wife's and the family's for future charity and scholarship giving. He wanted his children to be the trustees after his and his wife's passing. He did exactly that, but after all he was a man of means, had money and now he was wanting to set up a lifetime income not only for himself but future generations.

With $292.5 Million remaining, he then turned to his children. Lindel had always told them—especially when his children let him and his wife know they are spending their inheritance—"Your inheritance is in life insurance and our home, not in cash." They seemed to be assured of having an inheritance after all his spending and enjoying his money with his wife. He would allow $5 million for each of his three children, to set up a trust as the owner of life policies on Lindel and his wife. The life policy would be paid in full, thus establishing it as a single pay policy needing no additional money and little attention until their deaths. Death benefits are not taxed, so in this case they could use the proceeds to take care of their inheritance taxes. He also wanted to give each child an annual maximum tax-exempt gift.

He then took a portion of the remaining $277.5 million and shared it with each of he and his wife's six siblings at $1 million each. He wanted them to be millionaires as well. He also would enjoy seeing what they do with the money, so a stipulation would be, share with us how you spent it.

Now for the fun money. Lindel took the remaining $271.5 million and spent $2 million on a beautiful beach house in the Orange Beach/Gulf Shores Alabama area. It was a quick 6-hour drive, or even quicker plane ride, from their current home to the airport and a waiting car to be permanently parked there. As with all his toys, he wanted them to be carefree, needing little or no labor, and bring in income to the trust that owns it. This would mean a property manager. Rental dates would have to allow for family members' use of the beach house.

He then took the $269.5 million and invested $35 million in tax-exempt bonds. He felt he would need some advice on this, of course, but he likes municipal bonds and the like. He also spent another $15 million on physical silver and gold U.S. Eagle coins. Any profit on the sale of these would not be tax exempt but would be treated as capital gains. That hurts, but it was mainly a financial survival move and he likes coins.

Real estate. Most likely forest or farmland. Farmland, because of fewer renters, and forest, no renters. He said this would be a $19 million purchase, again with a property manager to watch over it. He said his main goal is to have everything hands-free and nothing to keep him tied down.

The remaining $150 of the $200 million he planned to be divided into smaller portions and placed into S&P Index funded life policies, IRAs and interest-bearing accounts. Again, he would need some guidance on this as well as some time to get it all in place. He wanted to keep some of the money available should an interesting investment or purchase come up.

The remaining $50 million would pay off all debts and purchase three automobiles and three boats. He always wanted a Maserati for sport, a new Suburban for travel, and to grant his wife's wishes for a third car. He then purchased a pontoon boat for leisure, a pleasure boat for recreation, and a fishing boat should he ever return to fishing.

Lindel always wanted to purchase a barrel of bourbon and have it custom labeled for him as gifts. This is costly, about $35,000, but well worth it for a bourbon lover.

He then turned to paying off his children's homes and assisted his three children in starting their own business.

Continuing his travels was a priority as well. "The world is a book and those that do not travel read only one page," said St. Augustine. Lindel and his wife had been fortunate to have traveled, and because of it he is a great believer in the words of St Augustine. He would like to continue reading the book.

He would return to some places, travel to some places they have yet to enjoy, and discover new destinations. He has his favorites like Italy, which his wife didn't care for, and she has her favorites which include the island of Oahu, Charleston S.C., and Boston. They agree on her three as well as British Columbia, most of the Caribbean Islands and San Diego. These they would return to. Places they missed along the way were Paris, Spain, Bermuda and Switzerland. They had been next door to these places, may have even passed through their airports, but were unable to spend time there. They would also like to return to Vancouver, Victoria and continue to Alaska on a cruise. Of course, they would want to continue their annual cabin trips with the siblings, seeing family in Texas, Oklahoma and Arkansas, their pleasure trips to the beach, Nashville and the Bourbon Trail in Kentucky.

All these things are great, but in the back of his mind Lindel knows there is more to life than monetary wealth. He knows you can have all these things and your family can have all these things, but if you do not have your health, there will be no enjoyment of life. Maintaining your health is important and money must be allocated for regular checkups, follow-ups, medication, healthy diet and exercise. It is a pain, time consuming and a constant interruption, but staying focused and on track is essential if you are to enjoy these wonderful gifts. Spending this money for better health prevention is vital. If you don't, you are just as at risk as people who can't afford health care, so in this case, there is no excuse for this.

George Bernard Shaw said, "The only person who behaves sensibly is my tailor. He takes new measurements every time he sees me. All the rest go on with their old measurements." Another thing we have touched on is protecting your wealth.

First, Lindel knows an annual review of all his finances are a must. Without this he will not know how he and his money are doing and where his is financially. It's part of his roadmap to his financial success. If you don't know where you are, how do you know how far you've come and where you are going? He must take measures and make decisions at least annually or more often if he feels the need.

Secondly, know those you have sought advice from. Can they be trusted? Did you check their background and references? Lindel knows we all change from time to time. Just think where you were a year ago and the changes in your life over that period. Be aware that those giving advice have also lived a year and had changes in their life. Be sure those changes won't affect their decisions and the advice they are giving.

Lindel is now retired with a lifetime income and is enjoying time with his wife, children and grandchildren. Businesswise, all things he planned for are in place and are running smoothly. This should help his family for generations. With his newfound freedom, he has the time and opportunity to teach them about both Golden Rules: "Do unto others as you would have them do unto you" and "The person with the gold makes all the rules". His hope is his family are the ones with the gold but treat others as they would want to be treated. No need to be a person of wealth and a complete horse's patoot.

CAN YOU TAKE IT WITH YOU?

Annette Cole Mastron

"You tried to bury me in life but all you did was unknowingly plant a seed in me. As Psalm 37:7 states, 'Rest in the LORD, and wait patiently for him: Fret not thyself because of him who prospereth in his way, because of the man who bringeth wicked devices to pass.' I've been waiting; now is my time. Patience is not inaction, but you never understood that. So I find the good in your goodbye, aunt."

This was my silent flawed eulogy I said over her black and white striped clad body before the casket was shut with a whoosh, clang, bang.

The trees had no clothes. I shivered watching the grave digger do his thing, filling back the grave of my last known relative. The service was nonexistent. There were no mourners. There was no service; she had long ago lost her faith. I had hoped she would see the light of redemption before she drew her last breath. Maybe she did at the very end. Only she and God would have that conversation. Now, she is gone from this world to suffer the consequences of her earthly actions. Stricken by a stroke prior to her death, she lost her mobility and her ability to scheme and deceive for the last weeks of her life, or so I surmised.

I rubbed unexpected tears away with the back of my hand before they froze. A wasted life of a talented but evil woman.

"Thank you, Mr. Reynolds, when will the headstone be placed?" I asked the undertaker, who appeared by the oak tree where the family plot is located.

"Not for about six weeks after the last freeze, so the ground can settle," Reynolds said.

"Please let me know when that happens so I can come to see it placed."

❧

I arrived home to unexpected guests. The doors of a black SUV opened, and four men exited and approached. I parked in the driveway but left my vehicle running. Two of the men came to the drivers' door and motioned for me to roll down my window. I powered it down a smidge and they handed me business cards with raised letters.

The tall one, Samson, asked, "Are you Senator Hilda Hawthorn's niece?"

"I was, she's dead and buried, as of two hours ago."

"We need to talk to you," the mustached one said. His name was Hitchcock, like the Psycho director, fitting.

"Look, I haven't been in contact with my aunt since I was fifteen. I was not involved with her life. If you want to talk to me further please contact my attorney, Gary Hays. I learned a long time ago, when it comes to my aunt's affairs, I must always be cautious. Now, please leave my home; it's been a long day."

I waited until they left and entered my cottage haven. I opened and shut the mission door, sighed and thought, "There really is no place like home."

I turned on Billy Joel and his "Italian Restaurant". The musical tale drifted throughout my home as I walked into the kitchen, opened the fridge and pulled out a bottle of wine. I poured a glass and wandered to my greenhouse office. I sat at my desk and logged on to my laptop, googling the names of the two mystery men. I found them on the Internet and they appeared to be who they said they were. Why would the Secret Service and Smithsonian want to talk to me?

Before I could muse further, my phone barked at me. I took a sip of wine as I picked up the phone. "Daisy, are you okay after today? Are you sitting down? You are not going to believe what I have to tell you."

"I'm fine, Gary. I'm sitting, nursing a glass of Chardonnay."

"Well," he continues. "I'll pick up some Thai food from Mosa and be at your place in thirty minutes. We need to talk in person about what I found out. See ya soon." He disconnected and I sipped some more wine, staring at the ancient treasure map of The Valley of Anchor framed above my desk. Next to it is the mounted shovel engraved with my parents' greatest Holy Land discovery.

Gary Hays is my best friend; he has known me since before I lost my parents. He's also my attorney. Cryptic, he normally is not.

Gary arrived with food boxes and chop sticks and carried everything into the library. I remoted on the gas fireplace and flames danced while the room filled with heat. I filled wine glasses. Billy Joel sang but he was now in a "New York State of Mind". We devoured the food in pleasant silence, passing the containers between us until we could eat no more. We toasted the fortune cookies.

"Read yours," I said.

Gary read, "You will embark on a journey that will bring you great fortune. Your turn, Daisy."

Mine read, "Great fortune is near."

"Are you up to talking or are you done for today?" he asked.

"You know me; let's get it all out so I can think about everything and start fresh tomorrow," I said.

"I got a call from Kevin Links, the attorney for your aunt. Apparently, you are her only heir."

"How is that possible? She resented me my whole life, especially since I wasn't on the boat with my parents when it blew up. She used my trust fund to forward her campaign for the Senate. She dumped me like trash. If your parents hadn't taken me in, I'd have been a ward of the state. She was a talented but hateful, evil woman. For gosh stakes, I'm still paying off my grad school student loans! She never helped me, emotionally or financially. Why would she leave me anything, she hated me. I figured she'd leave her ill-gotten money to a dog, like that dog in Switzerland. What's his name, we watched the docudrama for a second."

"You're talking about the Netflix show *Gunther's Millions*, about Gunther VI, the German Shepherd who inherited an estate of over $400 million. Like he knows what is done with the cash."

"Exactly my point. Why leave it to me unless she is trying to make a point from the grave."

"Links says the estate is substantial. Maybe a couple of million."

"This is totally out of character for her; there's bound to be a catch."

"Well, there's a letter from her. He wants us to meet him tomorrow in DC at her townhouse."

"You mean my parent's townhouse that she confiscated. As you know, I was fifteen when I invaded your home in Bethesda. I love your parents and so miss your Mom. Gone way too soon. Say, did you get a call from the Secret Service? Four guys were waiting on me when I got home. I told them to call you."

"Daisy," the letter stated, "solve the puzzle, like your parents didn't and it can all be yours. I'm thinking you're like your father, brilliant but not as smart as me, or like your mother, a puzzle solver, but I'm better than she ever was. I bet over the years you figured out that I killed your parents to get your trust fund. Did you know they had just discovered the location of another treasure? I recovered that treasure in secret. What cash and property I leave to you is nothing compared to the treasure you never knew about. So solve the puzzle or I will take it with me."

I sat in the leather wingback chair in my parents' previous home, holding my aunt's letter written on her embossed monogram stationary. I struggled to digest the diatribe of words of a truly vengeful wicked woman, clawing at me from the grave. What the heck? She leaves a letter that confesses to two murders and taunts me with promises of treasure. Her last chance to inflict pain, her favorite game.

I looked at Attorney Links, who was talking to Gary about the Nationals' chances for the upcoming season.

"Excuse me, did she leave anything else?"

Attorney Links went into attorney mode. His monotone voice stated, "Her estate and property total $6 million but she has outstanding debt of $3.5 million. With inheritance taxes you'll be lucky to get a million after all is said and done. The Secret Service want to inspect her properties for any items that need to be returned to the National Archives or Smithsonian. Your aunt borrowed some items for an event. Naturally, they want them back."

"What dress did she borrow? Let me guess—Jackie Kennedy's pink suit?"

"Well, that would have never been allowed," he said, frowning at me like I had three heads. "She borrowed a dress of Mary Todd Lincoln's and they want it back."

"Geez, like that's any better? How would I know where it is? The archaeologist in her had always been fascinated with the First Ladies. She even bought Mary Todd Lincoln's opera glasses at a Christie's auction years ago. What did the dress look like?"

"It was a black and white striped dress she wore it on that fateful night at Ford's theater."

"Oh my word, she didn't, did she? Boys, I think we're going to have to exhume a body. Yuck."

Both attorneys just stared at me, saying nothing, which is not like attorneys.

❧

Exhuming a body is not a fun way to spend the day. With both attorneys, mine and hers, two Secret Service men and two Smithsonian men at my side, the grave of my aunt was uncovered. The deed done, we followed the casket held by a truck crane to the cemetery's work shed, not the posh cemetery parlor. Can't get dirt on those antique oriental rugs. It would be too hard to explain. Plus, my aunt doesn't deserve nice because she wasn't. I felt like she was enjoying all the hoopla and laughing from Hell.

Mr. Reynolds kept discreetly looking in our direction, clearly not knowing what to say.

The casket was opened. We all approached. I took out my phone and saw that she was indeed wearing Mary Todd Lincoln's dress. I looked it up last night via Google. Mary was photographed at

Matthew Brady's studio in this dress prior to that night at Ford's Theater. In her hands, my aunt was holding Mary's gold opera glasses with a nosegay of decaying roses and purple pansies, like those Mary Todd Lincoln was fond of.

I turned. "Mr. Reynolds, when I viewed my aunt she didn't look like that. Why is she wearing a flower bed on her head?"

"I'm embarrassed to say but when I checked off your aunt's prepaid requests, I realized they hadn't completed everything on her list. I reopened her casket and positioned them as she requested. She provided a drawing of how she wanted everything placed. There was a problem, I'm sad to say—we could not insert the hoop undergarment. It was too wide for the casket."

"Where is the crinoline hoop? Please bring it here with all of my aunt's file and anything else. You can forward me all email correspondence between you and my aunt to my email. Here's my card with my email address. Thanks."

While Reynolds was gone, everyone took pictures of the casket with my dead aunt in all her stolen glory, playing like she was Mary Todd Lincoln, presumably. I knew my aunt was mean, crazy like a fox, but this is a whole elevated kind of disturbed. Wonder what her coordinated premeditated puzzle plan is trying not to tell me.

I looked at everyone and said, "Look, she's already dead. I'm telling you let's just do it and get her buried once and for all. Let's make sure we get this right so we don't have to do this again. She came into this world naked and she's gonna be buried naked. Just like 1 Timothy 6:7 says, 'For we brought nothing into this world, and it is certain we can carry nothing out.'"

The Smithsonian guys carefully removed the assassination night dress. It was laid out on a tarp and inspected. Everyone put on CSI gloves and felt in hems, seams, ruffles and embroidery for anything she may have hidden within the dress. Nothing was found in the dress.

"Okay, let's check out the opera glasses. Next, the shoes and silk stockings of Lincoln's era, then the nosegay and flower head piece."

The Smithsonian guys gleefully attacked the chores I outlined. Opera glasses, nothing. The attorneys plucked the flowers out of her casket and the flower shredding began. The dissecting continued. I walked to the head of the casket, lost in my thoughts. I pulled out her letter, reading and looking into the casket. I got nothing.

"Hey, look!" Gary yelled. "The comb holding the flowers is a Capitol locker key, number 321, look at the logo." I glanced at it and took a picture of the key.

Handing the 321 key to the Secret Service guys, I asked, "Can you guys check this out?"

Samson said, "I'll go, but he stays."

"Alrighty." I looked at the casket and said, "That's too easy, aunt, isn't it?"

"Whoa, the shoe heels have something in them!" Hitchcock exclaimed. "They are full of diamonds." I glimpsed the glittering pile of two hundred-plus diamonds of varying carat sizes. I took pictures, as did everyone else.

"I think we need to X-ray her body to make sure nothing else is hiding. Anyone know how to do this? I'm sure there are laws that need to be followed."

Attorney Links said, "I can supervise getting the body X-rayed but we will need to proceed with Reynolds' help."

Reynolds arrived carrying a paper file and a garment bag containing the crinoline hoop skirt. I took everything from him and set up in the corner where I could watch the goings-on while scouring through Reynolds' files on my aunt.

"Can y'all look at this hoop skirt?" I asked the Smithsonian guys. "This doesn't look like a period piece. It looks like something from a Halloween shop for a Southern belle outfit. What do you think?"

"It's not a period piece, not part of the dress. You're right, it's probably from the 1960s." They sounded disappointed.

I put the hoop back in the garment bag with my aunt's file and zipped it closed.

Gary was busy working on his iPad. He created an inventory complete with pictures. He created receipts for the Smithsonian guys to sign for what they are taking with them and holding me harmless.

Samson arrived. "Good news, the Capitol locker held the files the National Archives had been trying to retrieve from your aunt since she retired from the Senate. Our job here is done. Thanks for an interesting day and for being more cooperative than your aunt. Good luck, Daisy Hawthorn."

❧

Eighteen months later, after taxes and probate was complete, Gary inquired, "How ya doing?"

"I'm better than good. To quote Tony the Tiger, I'm great! I'm looking forward to attending the Mary Todd Lincoln exhibit featuring the previously stolen dress."

We lunched on my new-to-me boat, anchored at the Potomac Yacht Club in a slip next to a Senator who lives on his boat when he's in town. My left hand glittered with an oval cut diamond. Yes, one of the "heel diamonds." I gave it to Gary, who had it set in an art deco style ring. He got down on one knee, handed me a signed pre-nup and ask me to marry him. I said yes.

X-rays of Aunt Hilda's body showed no additional treasure. The diamonds were worth a cool $10 million after taxes.

❧

After the exhibition, Gary gave me a kiss. "Sorry I can't stay tonight but I have AM court tomorrow."

"No worries, I'll see ya tomorrow night." I exited the Uber and opened the townhouse. I waved at Gary as I locked the door and reset the alarm. I headed to the library, went to the mini fridge and pulled out a bottle of Chardonnay. I hit my phone app and Billy Joel's "Stiletto" began its methodical notes drifting through the rooms.

I took a sip of wine, lifted up my childhood copy of *The Secret Garden*, pressed the hidden button under it, and a wall of books slid open, motion lights clicking on as I descended down the stairs to the hidden room. I unlocked the steel grid door and entered my parents' safe room.

My aunt clearly never found it or knew about it. If she had, none of the gold from the Valley of Anchor would still be here. The crinoline hoop is in a stage of dissection and a hinged glass shadow box table glitters with pearls, doubloons, rubies, sapphires and emeralds. My aunt's treasure was sewn into the satin covered wire supports and hem of the hoop. I continue to laugh at my aunt's attempt to take it with her.

I've learned from this unusual experience. Waiting on God's timing is always key, along with knowing in your soul that truth has a way of rising to the top and overcoming evil. For now, I have my secret treasure and will share it when the timing is right.

A SHADOW'S TURN
John Burgette

Mr. Dawson and I were watching the aurora. The sky was much more active than what I had remembered from my Alaskan survival training. Before an ever-changing, flowing curtain of green, waves of blue and red colors washed across the sky. Occasional bolts of multicolored lighting trickled across a group of eastern clouds. There was no sound of thunder—only the swell of the ocean whispered along the tropical shoreline. Swoosh. Whoosh. From behind the dark silhouette of palm trees, Mr. Dawson and I watched the glowing sky.

To my right, I heard the rustling of leaves. Reflexively, I stepped forward and leaned into my left foot, pulled the gun strap away from my shoulder, and dropping the rifle into my hands, I turned and pointed the gun toward the sound. Mr. Dawson stepped back and laughed nervously.

"Whoa, pardner! It's likely some birds or a wild boar."

I nodded as I slowly placed the strap back on my shoulder. It was my job. I had been Mr. Dawson's bodyguard for several years. Before moving to the island, I had watched everything—every movement. I listened and reacted to all sounds. Large crowds demanded great attention. There are many movements and sounds in a crowd. The island hadn't been as challenging, especially now. Still, I followed Mr. Dawson everywhere. He had decided to go look at the sky, and I followed him. Everywhere—I followed him like a shadow. It was my job.

I glanced back toward the dark shadow of the mansion. I saw the flicker of orange flames where the campfire roared, as well as a smaller light from the cook's station. Otherwise, the island was dark. It always seemed dark. The only lights that shined over the island was the sun, the moon, the stars, and the aurora—above the darkness.

❦

Not long before, the island had been brighter … and louder. Rarely was there not pandemonium. It was a circus, and it had many performers. There were the socialites, the salespeople, the shysters, the playboys, the philanderers, the personalities, and the psychics— all competing for Mr. Dawson's attention. There were the grifters, gamblers, and gougers. There were the investors, the inventors, the intellectuals, and more salespeople—all wrangling for Mr. Dawson's fortune. It reminded me of the story when Moses climbed Mount Sinai, while the Israelites danced around the golden calf—except that Mr. Dawson was the golden calf.

There seemed to be many women, too, who wanted Mr. Dawson's attention. He was polite, but otherwise paid little notice of their humbug. Apparently, there was also a princess—I never learned if she was really a princess—who wouldn't allow his disregard to dissuade her.

I understood Mr. Dawson had not always been rich. For most of his life, he had struggled to pay bills, rent, and just live. When not working hard—long hours—he tried to stay warm in the winter and to feel solace in the summer. Then, unexpectedly, he fell into the huge fortune.

Fortunately, he was joined by a team of honest investors, who grew the fortune even greater. The team hired me to be his bodyguard—to protect him from harm. Only a few miles from where he had struggled to survive, he moved to a huge mansion, a complex … an institution. He was safe, but harm can appear in many ways, including unhappiness. Mr. Dawson was very unhappy in the mansion, in the complex, in the city. He announced that he wanted to live on an island.

The island held much promise. With nearly unlimited resources, a mansion was built with all the latest gadgetry. Huge generators were constructed, and many acres of solar panels were aligned along the east side of the island. Along with a marina, an airport was built.

The mansion had many servants and a world-renowned cook,

who was referred to as *The Cook*. Beyond the mansion was a farm for animals, which was managed by *The Farmer*. There was also a huge vegetable garden, which *The Gardener* managed. Each area had a staff, both inside and outside the mansion. It all seemed self-sustaining. It had become another complex. Still, Mr. Dawson seemed happy with the lifestyle, until the visitors began to arrive—then, more visitors began to appear.

Many guests seemed to have moved to the island, and they resided in one of the sundry, spare suites in the mansion. Though a few were entertaining, most were annoying, but none seemed dangerous to me. So, whoever Mr. Dawson allowed to stay on the island was his business.

One of the guests, who I learned to respect, was the CEO of an A.I. troubleshooting company. Although he, too, exploited the many amenities of the island complex, if it hadn't been for him, we might not have heard about *Icarus*.

Because his business partnered with many large science centers, the CEO was briefed by his research consultants about an urgent—and secret—high-level meeting. Joining the meeting virtually from the island, he invited Mr. Dawson and me (his constant shadow) to attend, but advised us to just sit in the corner and listen, along with his bodyguard. We weren't officially supposed to know about it, but the CEO sensed Mr. Dawson would need to understand what was soon to happen.

The meeting had much yelling, accusations, weeping, and nervous giggles. From what I could see from the video feed—which flickered and had constant delays—there were a lot of random movements and gestures. As a bodyguard, I was glad we were attending it virtually. There were many topics discussed, but a solar storm and its impact on the Earth were the most relevant to us.

I'm not sure how or why it happened, but there was a solar storm on the sun, and its impact would hit the earth in about three days or so. Through all the disagreements, a general consensus seemed to be that this storm—they named it Icarus—was a multi-year event. However, nobody seemed to know if it would be a few years or a few centuries. Discussing the impact from the storm generated the most emotion. I wasn't clear about some of the scientific jargon, but in short, Icarus would wipe out all power grids, electronic devices, etc.—humanity would turn medieval in a few days with no clear path back to "civilization."

Even though the attendees were sworn to secrecy—until they had developed mitigation plans—Mr. Dawson quickly organized an island-wide gathering to announce the problem and discuss options. Most people wanted to leave the island … immediately. Focused on escape plans, only a few seemed interested in checking with friends and family back home.

Most people were panicked, and the operation moved like a controlled commotion. A quick escape back to old communities was the simple goal, particularly for the visitors—particularly, the socialites, the shysters, the playboys, the philanderers, the personalities, the grifters, gamblers, and gougers. A few salespeople, intellectuals, and inventors, as well as one psychic, decided to stay on the island. Many of the staff decided to leave, too. Because most of the guests had their own yachts or private jets—there was enough room for staff, too—the exodus finished in less than a day. The princess was the first to leave.

What happened to those who fled, I'm afraid I don't know—with one exception. The CEO told us he wanted to just relax and enjoy the island, while he still could. He was very positive and jovial.

"Besides … in a few days, who will have a need for anything to do with artificial intelligence?"

Occasionally, I'd see him checking an old compass. He showed us how it was already jiggling back-and-forth a little. He said the moment it reached a certain point, then he'd still have several hours to safely fly his private jet to an international airport. I wasn't confident anything he said about the compass was true.

Eventually, he came to say goodbye, and we accompanied him and his bodyguard to the airport. His bodyguard, who was also his pilot, started the engines.

Before entering the jet, the CEO happily waved back at us and yelled, "Good luck! I hope you find what you need … here on this island."

As it climbed, the jet headed toward the west, but then began to circle toward the east while it continued to ascend. Suddenly, its wing lights disappeared as it quickly began spiraling into circles and spinning while it descended. In the last few seconds, it seemed to pull out of its dive as it crashed into the western cliffs off the island. A huge ball of orange, red, and blue flames drifted above the cliffs. In a few seconds, I felt a draft of hot air from the explosion.

Instinctively, I reached for my walkie-talkie to call our main office for any remaining staff to help us with a rescue along the cliffs. The radio was dead. My watch was not working. The outside lights were out. Apparently, Icarus had arrived.

Immediately, we all had to adjust—developing new roles and learning new skills. Because the Farmer had left, the Gardener had to lead the animal husbandry area, too. Some of the servants quickly adjusted, while others took some time for adapting to this new system. The few remaining guests seemed lost, but eventually, they often had the most original, problem-solving ideas.

All of the Cook's recipes had been on a computer tablet, and he had to work from memory. The kitchen was mostly useless, and he had to adjust—preparing meals on an open fire. In little time, other islanders designed and built better ways for him to cook, including a clay oven. Still, the Cook often seemed frustrated, and he could occasionally be heard to yell at the fire or oven—"Feu stupide!"

Before the storm, a handgun was the logical accessory for a bodyguard. Now, a rifle made more sense, because hunting became a new need. However, I carried it everywhere, because it was still my job to be Mr. Dawson's shadow.

∾

As we continued to watch the storm's spectrum of colors, Mr. Dawson asked me, "You OK? You happy you stayed?"

I offered my automatic answer, "It's my job," before I added, "I had nowhere else to go."

"I'm sure glad you stayed—that's for sure. You're a good hunter.

You got talent for build'n furniture and fix'n things to be used in new ways. … Yeah, I had no family and friends before all that money … then, there were too many of 'em."

I asked, "What about you … are you happy you stayed?"

Mr. Dawson straightened up tall, and he laughed. He told me how he had always dreamed of living on a tropical island. He told me how he liked the idea of starting fresh and doing things differently with a small group of people. He told me that this was his dream come true. Before the fortune found him, he liked to go to the library and read all the old stories about living on a desert island.

It was a fleeting thought, but I just started laughing. I laughed like I hadn't laughed in years. I had trouble stopping. I bent over a bit and laughed. I felt tears form in my eyes. I think I laughed for a minute or more. When I finally stopped, I stood stiff and said, "I'm … sorry."

He stepped back with his hands on his hips, smiled, and said, "Ain't nothing to be sorry about … kind'a refreshin'!"

We then returned to the campfire. Everyone was there. Over to one side, there were a few people singing—one was playing an acoustic guitar. The song was based on an old, heavy-metal rock tune, but their version sounded more melodic and gentle.

As he'd been doing for the last few days, Mr. Dawson sat next to the Gardener. They seemed very relaxed, and I saw an honesty and friendship between them that the princess could have never faked. He smiled and then asked for her first name.

"My name is … Grace. … It's funny, but few people, here, seem to speak each other's first name. I guess I was always afraid of asking you, the boss … your name."

Mr. Dawson paused, and as he scanned the people around the fire, he said, "You know, you're right about that. It isn't right we did it that way … just ain't right. … My name's Devlin."

He then stood up and announced, "Hey everyone! I just wanted ya'll to know. I ain't no boss no more. Things are changin'. We're all just folks, here … helpin' each other out—right? So, let's start by introducin' each other. … Shoot, even that storm has a name!

… My name's Devlin. What about ya'll?"

Each of the people said their names. Beside Danny and Grace, there were Esperanza, Julia, and Ben. And so it happened—names continued to be declared along the circle of people. One of the last to announce his name was the Cook—he was Benoit. That was it. The old titles and roles were gone—something new was happening.

I immediately loosened the rifle from my shoulder, removed its ammunition, and stood the empty gun next to a tree. As I stepped back, years of tension lifted from my shoulders.

Smiling, I looked at Devlin and said, "I guess, now, I don't need to be carrying *that* all the time."

He nodded and grinned, while Grace said, "So, we didn't get your name."

Looking back at Devlin, I said, "Believe it not … my name is Friday."

Devlin gawked at me, and then we both laughed. We kept laughing, and though she first looked puzzled, Grace started to chuckle, too.

"I'm going to take a walk," I said, and without waiting for a reply, I turned and walked toward the ocean.

I moved down the path toward the beach. I walked faster. I felt light and free. I was no longer a shadow. Although it was nighttime, I now noticed the different colors of the jungle, which flickered from the light of the campfire. The wind whispering through the trees, birds of the night, frogs, and insects—the sounds I had learned to ignore—surrounded me. Faster, I ran until I reached the ocean. On the beach, I stopped, removed my boots, and then slowly waded into the water.

I moved toward the open ocean, away from the island—just beyond its shadow. I stopped, and as the waves gently pushed against me, I watched the aurora in the sky, connecting with the water's reflection—moving, swirling, and enfolding my vision. I wept. I laughed. It engulfed me, and I embraced it all—colors from the sky, the warmth from the water, and the sounds of the night. I felt hopeful. Something new was happening … something good.

THE STASH
Ronald Lloyd

Raising his hand, Lyn Vasher tapped lightly on his grandmother's front door. When no one responded, he tapped a second time and was relieved to hear footsteps approach. As the door opened, he saw his mother peer out, finger to her lips. "Shush, Grandmother is sleeping."

Turning, Lyn's mother led him across the small living room and down a narrow hall to a white wooden door. As she put her hand on the knob, Lyn asked, "How is he?"

Pausing, Lyn's mother shook her head. "Not good."

Opening the door, the matronly woman led Lyn into a small room dominated by an iron bedstead. Lyn saw his uncle on the bed. His eyes were closed, his lower face covered with stubble and his chest heaving as he labored to breathe. Automatically, Lyn glanced up and compared the man before him with the picture on the dresser. His uncle looked so different from the uniformed eighteen-year-old on his way to save the world from the Nazi horde.

With a shake of her head, Lyn's mother lamented, "So sad. He had gone all the way across Europe only to be shot two days before the war's end."

Nodding, Lyn remembered the day his uncle had come home, a large bandage protruding from under the collar of his shirt. The doctors had assured the family that he was recovering, but his uncle had weakened by the month instead of strengthening. After several-dozen visits to the VA, the doctors could only shake their heads, assuring the family they had done all they could.

Hearing his uncle mumble, Lyn leaned forward. "What did you say, Uncle Eric?"

Feeling his mother's hand on his shoulder, Lyn pivoted and saw her hopeless expression. "He's been delirious all afternoon, muttering something about being a millionaire and finding gold in the forest. Nothing that makes any sense."

Turning to leave, Lyn's mother said, "I will be in the guest bedroom. If anything changes, wake your grandmother and me."

Taking a chair by the foot of the bed so he could see his uncle, Lyn picked up the book he had begun the night before. As time passed, his uncle continued to mumble and move fitfully until shortly before two o'clock in the morning.

Roused by the silence, Lyn lowered his book and saw his uncle's eyes were fixed on him.

"Yes, Uncle. Do you need something?"

"I ain't gonna make it."

"Don't say that. You're going to be fine."

"No, but I have something for you."

"What is it?"

Raising a feeble hand, the dying man pointed at his closet. "Over there. Get my uniform tunic."

Rising, Lyn laid his book on the foot of the bed as he turned to the closet, where he found his uncle's army uniform on a hanger and a pistol belt draped around it. In the holster, Lyn saw the butt of the Luger his uncle had brought back from the war.

Removing the pistol, Lyn laid it on the nightstand and, holding the uniform up, asked, "Is this what you wanted?"

His finger shaking with the effort, Lyn's uncle pointed. "Open the jacket. I have hidden a paper in the lining."

Exhausted, Lyn's uncle dropped his hand as Lyn probed inside a small rip. Feeling the edge of a folded sheet of paper, Lyn extracted it. "Uncle, what is this?"

"Have you ever heard of the Werwolf?"

Shaking his head, Lyn said, "Don't think so."

"It is German for werewolf. It was a guerrilla force the Nazis planned to use after the fall of Germany. In the last days of the war, the Nazis stashed weapons and such all over the country, but that's not all. They also hid gold to fund the resistance.

"Two days before the end of the war, I captured one of the Werwolf commanders. He had a paper on him with the coordinates to a cache of gold. When he resisted, I killed him but not before he shot me."

Pausing, Lyn's uncle took a moment to regain his strength before continuing. "The army sent me to the States for treatment before I could dig up the stash. I have been planning to go back ever since, but now that's not going to happen."

Raising a feeble finger, the dying man pointed to the paper. "All my plans, the location of the gold, my contacts in Germany and everything you'll need to get the stash out of Germany are on the paper.

"Give a third of it to my mom and a third to your mother. You can have the rest. But don't give anything to that good-for-nothing ex-wife of mine. Let one of those fellows she ran around with when I was overseas take care of her."

His mind overflowing with questions, Lyn looked down but saw his uncle's eyes had closed. Two hours later, never rousing again, his uncle died.

∾

As Lyn descended the stairs of his airplane to the tarmac of the Dresden Airport, his hand reflexively rose to pat the breast pocket of his shirt. Reassured by the slight bulge of his uncle's paper, Lyn saw a sign in German, Russian, and English. It read "Customs".

Reminding himself to remain calm, Lyn approached a man in a shabby uniform and extended his passport. Taking the small booklet with the American eagle on the cover, the man opened it and compared the picture on the inside with Lyn. "Was ist der grund besuchs?" Seeing Lyn's puzzled look, he said, "What is the purpose of your visit?"

"Oh, uh, I am a doctoral student at Memphis State Teachers' College, and I am here to do research for my dissertation. I will be at the university for five days and then go to Charles University in Prague to continue my research."

With a bored nod, the official lifted a stamp, inked it on a pad, and brought it down with a sharp blow on the first blank page of Lyn's passport. Handing the booklet back, he announced in a dull voice, "Welcome to the Russian zone of occupation, Mr. George King. Enjoy your stay."

Resisting the impulse to sigh with relief, Lyn asked for directions to the baggage claim. After only one wrong turn, he emerged into a long hall. Stopping a pace inside the door, Lyn glanced to his right and left, finding suitcases and garment bags piled up and down the room's length. Unsure where to go, he approached a man with an airline logo on his shoulder and presented his baggage-claim ticket.

Without a word, the man pointed down the hall where Lyn saw two men bringing luggage in from the tarmac. After Lyn presented his claim ticket a second time, one of the men searched the pile and retrieved his suitcase. Grabbing the bag's handle, Lyn lifted it but stopped when he felt one side sag and heard a loud clang.

His stomach clenching in fear, Lyn dropped the bag and, kneeling beside it, saw that the latch was broken. Raising the top, he swept the entrenching tool he had bought at an Army Surplus into the bag.

Encircling his luggage with both arms, Lyn rose and turned to see a large man with a flat face and long overcoat staring at him. Cradling the suitcase, Lyn ducked his head as he scurried out the main exit.

Once on the sidewalk, Lyn pivoted his head, searching for a cab. Seeing a line of taxis to his left, he raised his hand to attract their attention and was relieved when a Mercedes-Benz started toward him.

Looking down at the broken latch, Lyn thought, *"Strange, it's brand-new."* A moment later, fear gripped his gut as realization dawned. Someone had broken the latch and searched his bag.

Anxious to get away, Lyn stepped toward the approaching taxi, only to leap back as a battered pre-war Volkswagen suddenly appeared, turned in front of the Mercedes, and halted by the curb. With a blast of his horn, the Mercedes surged around the intruder and onto the next passenger.

Oblivious, the Volkswagen driver threw open his door and jumped out. Startled, Lyn hesitated and asked, "Do you speak English?"

As he opened the luggage compartment, the driver nodded, adding, "Ya. English goot."

Before Lyn could inquire further, the man grabbed his suitcase and deposited it in the luggage compartment, asking with a smile, "We go?"

As Lyn turned to get in the rear passenger seat, he saw the overcoat man standing on the sidewalk a dozen feet away. "Who's that man staring at me?" Lyn asked.

Turning to see, the driver whipped back around. "No look. KGB."

"KGB?"

Ignoring his question, the driver pointed to the door. "We go."

Once in the car, Lyn waited until the cabby was behind the wheel and then demanded, "What is the KGB?"

"KGB Russian secret, how you say, polizei."

"Police. You mean police?"

"Ya, ya, police."

As the car started with a pop and a stutter, the cabby said, "You no worry. Russian watch all American."

Turning in his seat, Lyn saw Overcoat Man scrutinizing them as his car pulled away from the curb. *If the cabby meant his words to be comforting, they weren't.*

Maneuvering through the ruined city, Lyn's driver asked, "Where go?"

✍

Four days later, Lyn slammed the door of his hotel room behind him and, after locking it, began to shake. For the second day in a row, he had seen Overcoat Man watching him. Stepping to the small table near the window, Lyn decided to move the plan up twenty-four hours, find the stash, and get out of the Russian occupation zone as quickly as possible.

Mentally, Lyn began to check off each step of the plan. Retrieving his uncle's paper from his pocket, he opened his bag and took out a map. Laying it on the bed, he found the coordinates and, using his finger, traced the route he would take the following day.

Reaching into the case, Lyn took two sets of clothes off the top, revealing three large, folded duffel bags. Opening one, he placed the other two duffels in it before adding the entrenching tool and a compass. Finally, he took three cartons of American cigarettes out of his bag (to use as bribes for the border guards) and laid them beside the tool.

Satisfied, Lyn flung himself, fully clothed, on the bed. Certain that he was too nervous to sleep, Lyn was surprised to awaken when the dawn's light came through the window.

After throwing water on his face, brushing his teeth, and scraping off a few whiskers, Lyn made his way to the hotel restaurant. He forced himself to eat a couple of pieces of toast and drink a cup of coffee. Then, he walked out to the street.

As usual, the driver of the battered Volkswagen was waiting for him at the curb. Standing, the man gave Lyn a cheery "Guten Morgen."

Handing the driver his suitcase, Lyn nodded and replied, "Good morning."

Keeping the duffel with him, Lyn sat in the rear seat as the cabby took his place behind the wheel and looked back questioningly. Leaning forward, Lyn pointed to a location on his map and said, "Go there." With a nod and a couple of "ya's," the two set off. In minutes, they were out of the city and climbing a series of hills.

When the car arrived at the coordinates, the driver stopped and again looked back at Lyn. On the hill to his right, Lyn saw a large rock outcrop, the first location noted in his uncle's instructions. Gesturing to a dirt road a hundred meters away, Lyn told the driver, "Pull in there so no one will see you."

Taking his duffel, Lyn climbed to the rock and, using his compass, walked thirty paces northwest. After sweeping away some leaves, he was relieved to find a rusted metal rod embedded in the ground.

Turning up the hill, Lyn continued to the top where he found a pile of rocks. Turning west again, he moved fifty paces to a small clearing. Dropping the duffel onto the ground, he took out the entrenching tool and, after unfolding it, strode to the middle of the clearing and began to dig. Within moments, he struck something hard and, dropping to his knees, eagerly scraped the dirt to the side, revealing the top of a rectangular metal box.

Lyn probed around the edge using his hands and found four rusted latches. Using the entrenching tool, he forced the fasteners open, and—after lifting the lid—he was rewarded with a golden glare. Exhilarated, he lifted one of the rectangular bars up, noticing the Nazi swastika on the top.

Focused on the gold brick, Lyn was startled when a gravelly voice said in German, "Was hast du gefunden?"

Lyn's head snapped around. He was horrified to find Overcoat Man pointing a pistol at him. Unable to understand, Lyn froze until the Russian flicked the gun's barrel upward. Once Lyn was on his feet, Overcoat Man gestured for him to step back. As Lyn inched backward, the Russian's attention turned to the box. He failed to notice as Lyn slipped his hand into his jacket pocket.

"Grosser Gott," Overcoat Man exclaimed and, with a greedy grin, pointed his gun at the American. Realizing he had only moments to live, Lyn didn't attempt to take his uncle's Luger out of his pocket.

Pulling the trigger, Lyn fired two shots through the cloth of his coat. The pistol's natural inaccuracy, increased by firing from the hip and through the fabric, sent the bullets wide of their target.

Startled, the Russian instinctively jumped back as Lyn leaped to seek shelter behind a large tree. Recovering his wits, Overcoat Man extended his pistol and fired.

Feeling the wooden trunk shiver with the impact of a bullet, Lyn thrust his gun around the tree and fired twice without looking. Using the shots as a distraction, Lyn bent low as he fled farther into the woods.

Ignoring the branches striking his face, Lyn careened from tree to tree as he raced down the far side of the hill. Hearing a bullet whine through the leaves to his right, he flung himself between two bushes and found only open air on the other side.

Twisting, Lyn sought to bring his feet under him but only half succeeded before he struck the bottom of the ravine. His fingers, loosened by the landing, let go of the Luger, sending it flying across the dry creek bed. Above him, Lyn saw the Russian silhouetted against the sky, his body assuming a shooter's stance and his pistol pointed at Lyn.

Desperate, Lyn lunged toward his Luger as a bang echoed through the forest. Sure that he had been shot, Lyn braced himself for the pain but, feeling nothing, looked up. Above him, the Russian's hands dropped, his gun falling onto the rocks beside Lyn. A heartbeat later, Overcoat Man tipped forward and landed beside the American.

In shock, Lyn didn't move until he saw the bushes part and the cabby's head emerge. Shaking in reaction, Lyn shouted, "What took you so long?"

Placing his gun in his pocket, the driver shrugged. "It's a tall hill."

SAVING DESTINY
Beth Krewson Carter

The first sign of trouble was the twilight sky. Jake was almost never late, especially when he had been working all day.

"C'mon," I muttered, heading outside to sit on the front steps. "Where are you?"

Lingering light faded on the horizon, so I dug a cigarette out of my pack. Thumbing my lighter, I blew smoke rings into the cool air and listened to the frogs start their springtime serenade. I was halfway through my Newport before my eyes stopped scanning the gravel road. If Jake didn't show up soon, I needed to get up and refrigerate the Hamburger Helper. I was just about ready to give up my vigil and head inside the trailer when the headlights of his truck bobbed in the distance.

"I'm going to be staying with a friend," Jake announced once we were both in the living room.

Confused, I followed him as he headed down the hallway. Without looking at me, he started packing a bag in the bedroom. His movements had a speed I rarely saw, as if he had already thought about every piece of clothing. When he finally turned to look at me, his eyes dropped to the floor.

"You can stay here until the end of the month but then you and Destiny need to be on your way."

At that moment, I realized that sitting in the dark waiting for my boyfriend had only meant one thing.

"So, you're leaving?" I asked, hating the way my voice sounded small when I was only surprised.

"Yeah, uh, sorry, Dylan, but you and me, we just don't click, you know? I get that things have been hard for you, and I feel bad about everything, but..."

He shrugged his scrawny shoulders and then headed out into the growing darkness. I was several feet behind him, but my body felt numb, so I stopped in the doorway. At the last minute, he finally looked back at me.

"Hey, don't mess with the furniture, but you can take some small stuff if you want."

I knew better than to cry, so I simply closed the door. In the stillness of the trailer, I sat on the sofa and listened to the sound of his truck engine fading into the night.

Even though I was upset, Jake's decision to go really wasn't a total surprise. In a way I kind of expected it because we weren't great together. The problem was that while neither of us was ever bad with each other, we weren't that good either. I guess you could say we were just marking time and even I know you can't build a future on a lukewarm relationship.

Besides our obvious lack of chemistry, I had also started to sense that I probably wasn't Jake's type. Girls like me, big boned and chunky, don't often hold much appeal for men. Of course, the fact that my hair is often frizzy didn't add a lot to my allure.

To my credit, whatever I lacked in runway beauty, I made up for in street smarts. Thanks to my youth spent in foster care, I always considered myself a master of reading moods and emotions. I was better than most at picking up on the clues of disenchantment, at least before Jake came into my life.

I guess having a boyfriend just made me comfortable. Up until he left, I would have probably said how much I liked living with Jake in his double wide. Back then, I thought Walnut, Mississippi was a pretty good place. I mean I wasn't unhappy or anything. Of course, it's not like everything was always so wonderful, because it wasn't, but when you you've lived in as many homes as I have, staying in one place, one bed, feels pretty good.

Besides the trailer, I also liked my job at the grocery store. My commute over the state line into Tennessee wasn't too bad and most of my coworkers were good people. The store manager knew I liked art, so he let me do all the signage for the Deli. I even got to purchase baked goods at an employee discount. Perks like bringing home extra cookies really made Destiny excited.

Other than work, I always knew most boyfriends wouldn't have been as easy going about my little sister. Destiny's the only family I have left. Jake understood how important she was to me so after I got permanent hours, he helped me petition to be her legal guardian. Naturally, it took a couple of months, but eventually she came to me for good. Since my trailer was so old, Jake suggested we all live at his place. Only after we moved in together did Destiny finally sleep without having nightmares. She still didn't talk much, but she seemed better, as if we were finally somewhere safe. Jake could have been impatient with Destiny, but he wasn't. He was always mellow, but I guess smoking weed most days will do that to you.

When I finally got off the sofa that night, I decided I might as well start packing. I went to the kitchen to look through cabinets. As I was pulling out dishes, I saw the lottery tickets on the counter. Just the sight of those games made me groan because they reminded me of Jake. He loved to gamble, so most weeks I'd gift him with a few different games purchased at the end of my shift.

I started to walk the whole stack to the trash can until something made me stop. Maybe I had a twinge of revenge. All I know is that before my fingers could talk to my brain, I grabbed one of the tickets and decided to do my own scratching. Only when I saw a five-figure winning number did my mouth go dry.

For the rest of the night, I didn't do anything but pace the floor and stare at my winning numbers. Fortunately, Destiny was asleep in the back of the trailer, so I used the time to come up with a plan.

In the morning, I put Destiny on the school bus the same as always, and then I got in my car and went to work. Nobody was expecting to see me since I was off on Wednesdays. Without being noticed, I headed for my manager's office.

As soon as he saw me, Big Earl, my boss, logged off his computer. I guess he could tell I needed to talk because he motioned for me to sit.

To most people, Big Earl looked scary, like some sort of chocolate colored mountain man. Thankfully, I knew from working with him that his heart was as big as his barrel chest. If anyone could be trusted, I knew he could.

"Well, aren't you the lucky one?" he said when I showed him my card.

"What do I do? I bought the ticket here, at the store."

Earl rubbed his beefy neck, lost in thought. "Well, this is a five-figure sum, so you'll need to go to the state office in Nashville to claim your prize."

"You won't say anything, will you? I don't want any publicity."

"Not about you, but our store will get credit for selling a winning ticket. That type of information I can't control, but I don't have to say who won."

For a minute, I was quiet, wondering if Big Earl would keep his word. To me, he had always been a good man who tried to do right by folks in town. Looking in his eyes, I decided to be honest.

"This money is going to let me give my sister the home she really needs. If word gets out that I won a lottery game, every foster home I ever lived in will find a way to come after me for a piece of this and I really need it for Destiny. Even if it means getting less money, I must keep this quiet."

Earl nodded his head and then leaned across his battered desk to catch my eye.

"After you get your money, why don't you think about leaving Middleton?" he asked in a low voice. "You're a great employee but I know you always wanted to do art and draw, and I bet you could head to Memphis. You and Destiny could start over with a new school for her and some classes for you, maybe at community college. If you wanted, I could even make calls to some stores in that area so you could work, too."

His suggestion was so heartfelt that a lump started forming in my throat. Say what you will, but after a lifetime of knowing bad people, the good ones stand out like jewels. With tears in my eyes, I smiled and nodded in appreciation.

Only after I went to Nashville and had the money wired to my savings, did I finally tell Destiny about the idea of moving.

"So, I'm thinking maybe we should consider a new place to live. Somewhere better, just for the two of us. I have some money now."

As usual, Destiny didn't say anything, and I wondered what she thought. Did the idea of moving frighten her? She had never even asked me about Jake, and I still didn't know whether she had figured out that he wasn't coming back to us.

On my last day at Kroger, I looked up from the end cap display I was creating to see my favorite person in the world. Miss Lilly Mae, my foster mom for two years, was pushing her cart in my direction and waving.

Of all the people I lived with as a teenager, Miss Lilly Mae was probably the best. When I needed a job in high school, she was the one who told Big Earl what a good girl I was. She even allowed me to stay with her and her husband, Harold, past my eighteenth birthday.

"This is your last day?" she asked, folding me into her pillowy body for a long hug. "Where're you going, child?"

"I'm headed to Memphis. Destiny lives with me now and I'm going to go to community college."

"Well, I'm real proud of you, Dylan. That news just makes my day. I always knew you were going to do big things."

She patted my hand and her touch felt so good. I stood there and soaked in her kindness the way a plant drinks in water.

"If you're going to be in Memphis," she continued, "I might call you sometime and visit. Harold lost his leg about six months ago and I take him to the VA Hospital there at the beginning of every month."

I must have looked concerned because Miss Lilly Mae reached out and touched my cheek.

"Harold's alright, don't you worry. The only problem he has right now is getting into our house. Those steps are hard, and he needs a ramp, but other than that he is fine."

She hugged me one last time before ambling down the next aisle. As I watched her go, my mind was already at work.

The next day, after loading up everything in my car, I was surprised by how few possessions we had.

"We'll get you a new bed as soon as we sign the lease and pick up the key," I promised my sister as we left the trailer park.

Destiny merely looked out the window. I tried to read her

expression, to see if she was excited, but all I could see was a little girl intent on studying the cotton fields slipping past us.

After a trip to IKEA and a week combing thrift stores, our apartment was furnished. Only then did I pick up the phone and called Miss Lilly Mae.

"Lawd, Dylan, is that you? So, tell me, are you in Memphis now?"

"Yes, I'm with my little sister Destiny."

"Well, I'm coming up there next week with Harold. He has a doctor's appointment at the VA. Maybe we could meet up with you and your sister. You know, we always try to eat somewhere after every appointment. Would the two if you be our guests at the Piccadilly Cafeteria before we drive back home?"

"We'd love to," I said, warmed by the offer. "So, how's Harold doing?"

"He's doing fine, especially now that we have a ramp. Oh, did I mention that we got the nicest wooden ramp? Would you believe, someone just sent a carpenter over to our house and had it built? The whole thing was such a surprise, and we don't even know who to thank."

The excitement in her voice made me smile. If ever a couple deserved to have manna from heaven, it was Miss Lilly Mae and Harold. That's when I realized that building a ramp for them was maybe one of the best parts of having money. Surely, there was nothing that had ever felt as rich as being able to give an anonymous gift to them.

I hung up the phone and settled down to look at my new laptop. For a few minutes, I was totally absorbed in the syllabus for my graphic design class until I heard something.

At first, the sound was so low, so I thought a pipe from the kitchen might be making noise. I rose from my seat, straining to hear until I figured out what was happening.

Destiny was singing.

In my whole life, I had rarely heard my sister talk, much less sing a song.

I followed the soft melody to her room. Destiny was under her

Taylor Swift blanket surrounded by stuffed animals.

"That's a pretty tune," I said.

A crooked smile transformed her face, but then she looked me dead in the eye and asked me question I wasn't expecting.

"Dylan, are we rich now?"

The look on my sister's face was so innocent that for a moment I was at a loss. All the wise answers, the ones I was supposed to have, simply evaporated.

How should I explain the difference between a fortune and being fortunate? In our case, what was a small windfall to some people changed our future and gave us a new life. The money I won gave me opportunities, but most importantly, it probably saved Destiny.

"Well, we are blessed to have some money in the bank, but we're more blessed to have each other and friends like Miss Lilly Mae and Harold who are coming to visit us," I told her.

I watched my sister as she weighed the ideas behind my answer. When she smiled again, I knew she understood. We kissed goodnight and I headed back to my computer.

For the rest of the night, until she fell asleep, I could hear Destiny singing.

ONE GOOD TURN
Frank DiBianca

My life is a train wreck too! Eddie Cangoods had been musing over the classic film he and his wife, Bella, watched yesterday, which was Christmas Day. Charles Dickens's *A Christmas Carol* starred Alistair Sim as Ebenezer Scrooge.

I'm thirty-seven years old. Been married fifteen years. Eddie, this is garbage pickup day!

Without hesitating, he hurried around the house and trashed his bottles of liquor and his adult magazines and videos, along with several erotic novels.

After collecting his thoughts, Eddie drove to his girlfriend's apartment and rang her bell. Tessie Nelson opened the door and smiled. "Hi, Eddie. Come on in." She sat on the love seat and motioned toward the empty half.

Still standing, Eddie said. "This will be easier for both of us if I get straight to the point. Christmas has awakened me. You mean a lot to me, Tessie, but I want to go on the straight and narrow from now on. I want—"

"Christmas, eh?" Tessie interrupted. "You been watching any Scrooge movies? You wanna talk here or in the bedroom?"

"Sorry, but I came here to separate, not arbitrate or copulate. I cannot continue this dual life. What we're doing is wrong. Tessie, I wish you every happiness. Goodbye, my friend."

She snapped her head away.

He walked back to the door. As he opened it, he heard, "Friends? Is that what you call the past five years? Don't make me…"

And the door closed on her sarcastic reply.

❧

On the ride home, Eddie's mind turned upbeat. Henceforward, he would incorporate God into all his thoughts. Focus on loving God and putting others ahead of himself. Look for opportunities to do good deeds. Read the Bible every day.

He felt good… free… like a monster barbell had been lifted from his shoulders. He couldn't wait to tell Bella the news.

"Hi, Bell," Eddie said as he walked into his wife's sculpture studio upstairs where she had just started shaping a slab of clay. "You'll love what's happened to me."

"Really? I'm all ears."

"It seems the Lord has answered your prayers of the past fifteen years."

Bella gasped and put her hand on a nearby table to steady herself. "Oh, Edward, I... I... Praise the Lord!! Just let me get this frock off, and we'll go to the den and talk."

After they'd reached their destination, Bella sat on the love seat, and Eddie swallowed hard and joined her.

"Tell me more." She asked.

"It started with the movie we watched yesterday. *The Christmas Carol* story was new to me, and it shocked me. I believe the Lord used the movie to show me how rotten my life was. I'd sensed that before, but this time, I want to do something about it."

Eddie summarized what had transpired, concentrating on his plans for reformation.

"This is the happiest day of my life since our wedding. Are you gonna come to church with me now?"

"Absolutely. And we can review their social and educational programs together. But now, will you give me this room for the rest of the day? I have a lot of reading and some praying to do."

They hugged and kissed more fervently than they had for many years. Then Bella went to their bedroom and poured out her heart to the Lord.

For six hours, Eddie read from the Bible and prayed. Halfway through this period, Bella knocked and asked Eddie if he wanted anything to eat.

"No thanks, hon, a little fasting will do me good."

At one point, he rose to jog on the treadmill and dropped the Bible. It landed face down and open. He picked the book up and turned it over. Acts, Chapter 9. He sat again and began reading. *This is amazing.*

☙

The next morning, Eddie woke up at 10:00 and read a note Bella had left on the kitchen table. "My Darling Eddie, I waited for you to come down. My heart is still bursting with joy over what you said last night, and I can't wait to hear more, but we need food for dinner. I left the coffee on warm."

Eddie poured a cup of coffee and took it to the den to reconsider everything. Yesterday, he'd scanned Genesis, followed by the story of Paul's conversion in Acts, and the four Gospels.

A loud triple rap on the front door interrupted the reverie filling Eddie's mind. He stood and hurried to open the door. *Nobody here. No delivery truck. This is weird.* After scrutinizing the street, he turned to go back in. Glancing down, Eddie spotted a beautiful, sky-blue business envelope with no markings on it.

He picked it up and rushed back to the kitchen table to open the envelope. Inside, a packet of ten hundred-dollar bills and a blue card with black letters reading "USE THESE FOR MY GLORY" froze his attention.

Soon, Bella returned, and Eddie related the previous day's and the morning's events. But the blue coloring of the mysterious packet they'd received had turned white, and the black letters were gone. The bills remain unchanged.

"A thousand dollars! It's a miracle if ever I saw one," Eddie exclaimed.

Bella was more measured. "It's fantastic! But I'd call it a blessing."

"Not a miracle? A knock on the door and seconds later, there's no one in sight? A thousand dollars from nowhere? Blue paper that changes to white? Ink that disappears?"

"Look, honey," Bella answered, "I treasure this wonderful time in our marriage, but let's consider the facts before we go supernatural. The vanishing delivery person could have run around the house and into the trees behind us. The money could be from a philanthropic believer with an overactive imagination. And delayed chemical reactions could explain the color changes."

"But why would anybody do the disappearing stuff? Chemical or spiritual, it's like they didn't want you to believe me or something."

"That's a good point. And they delivered it while I was out. Look, if you're convinced it's from the Lord, maybe you should decide what to do."

"Almost forgot to tell you I have to get my hair done at 1:00, and I have a bridge club meeting at 3:00. It's great we both have the holiday week off."

While Bella was away, Eddie took her advice and made a plan to use the money to honor God. He took his plan and the money to the supermarket and filled each of ten large shopping bags with identical $100 selections of cans, jars, and packaged foods. Then he filled the rear storage compartment of his SUV with the bags and headed down Mercy Drive, where panhandlers congregated. At the top of each bag, Eddie carefully placed a card reading "A GIFT OF FOOD FOR YOU FROM GOD. DO NOT SELL IT."

Eddie dropped off a bag everywhere a panhandler was located. "Praise the Lord!" one fellow cried out. "Now I can stay off the street for the rest of the week. Maybe give some to my buds."

A woman with a withered hand looked at him with tears in her eyes. She tried to speak but couldn't. Eddie gently took her deformed hand and kissed it.

Similar displays of gratitude at other stops warmed Eddie's heart, but one person just grinned, and after reading the card, shook his head. Another pulled his head back and frowned, and then tossed the card on the ground. After disbursing all ten bags, he closed the rear hatch and noticed there were two bags back in the storage area.

He drove on, scratching his head, and gave the bags away again. None came back this time.

&

When Eddie got home, his watch read 4:05, and his wife hadn't returned yet, so he went to the den and began reading Exodus. An hour later, Bella came in. "What a miserable afternoon. As soon as I sat down in the hair salon, I got a splitting headache. No fun playing bridge either. And my head's still pounding."

"Sorry to hear that, hon. Wanna hear what I did with the money?"

"I'd love to, but I'm completely exhausted and heading to bed. Maybe tomorrow."

&

The next day, Bella stayed home to observe in case the events repeated. Eddie summarized his food distribution the previous day, and just as they started a discussion, they heard three knocks. Bella suddenly got a strong urge to leave the room and had to hurry away, telling Eddie she'd be back as soon as possible.

This time there was a blue box with a hundred blue packets, each containing a hundred $100 bills. *100 x 100 x $100 equals a million dollars!* The box also contained a blue card reading "USE THIS AS YOU WISH." This time, Eddie played it safe and took several photos of the box's contents.

When Bella returned, her husband told her what had happened and showed her the money. Bella leaped and shouted, "We're rich! But look, everything is white again, and the words you described are gone again."

"Yeah, they were here before you arrived, but this time, I took pictures." Eddie pulled out his phone and cycled through the photos. But the blue coloring and the words had disappeared in the photos as well!

"And I ran around to the back of the house. Took me about ten seconds. Nobody there."

After much discussion about what to do next, they each made a list of how they would spend the money. Eddie's list proposed giving it all to the Lord. Bella wanted to tithe 10% to God and keep the rest.

"My way is the Biblical way," she contended. "God asks us for a tenth of our money, not all of it." Bella folded her hands for emphasis.

Eddie sat back in his chair. "We wouldn't be giving Him all of our money. Our combined income from our jobs is about $140,000, and we're living well on that, don't you think?"

"Yes, I do. But I still think He wouldn't have said 'Use this as you want to' if He intended us to give Him all of it. It just doesn't make sense."

"Look, hon, let's go into the kitchen, and I'll make us a pot of coffee. I think we need to review everything that happened. Maybe the Lord's given us a clue somewhere."

Bella nodded, and they strolled hand in hand to the kitchen. When they arrived, Eddie retrieved his laptop computer. He prepared the coffeemaker and sat alongside Bella at the kitchen table.

"The analysis we are about to do will only work if you believe every word I said and say now. I wasn't hypnotized. OK?" Eddie grasped Bella's hand and stared into her eyes. "So, let's examine the facts and see what questions and conclusions arise."

"Sounds good to me," Bella responded.

Eddie nodded, and they began working together to develop the list.

This is what they came up with.

The Strange Deliveries After Christmas

<u>Main events:</u>

1. I have a spiritual transformation that involves purification and

dedication of my life. You have always been pure and dedicated to God.

2. We get $1,000 in $100 bills with apparent instructions from God to use it for His glory while you are at the hairdresser and bridge club.

3. We discuss this. You leave it to me and head out. I buy a thousand dollars worth of food and deliver it to street panhandlers with notes that this is a gift from God.

4. The next morning, we get $1,000,000 in $100 bills with instructions to use it as we wish. You suddenly become indisposed and can't witness what happens.

5. We discuss use of the money. I say give it all to God. You say tithe it.

<u>Discussion topics:</u>

1. Lifestyles
2. Commitments
3. What is the Lord doing?

<u>Strange aspects:</u>

1. Disappearing delivery person (twice)
2. Blue paper becomes white (twice)
3. Disappearing Instructions (twice)
4. Delivered food bags transported back to my SUV (two bags)
5. Your absence from both deliveries

They thought about the list for a few minutes until Bella ventured a proposal. "How about if we adjourn for an hour, and think everything over? I believe more is here than just two people getting a weird cash bonanza."

Eddie nodded and took his laptop to his office upstairs. "I'll print out two copies of our list and bring you one." Bella headed to her sculpting studio.

An hour later, they reconvened in the den. Bella asked Eddie to go first.

"Sure. I'll read my responses.

"Lifestyles? Until the day after Christmas, mine stunk. Now I believe the Lord has me on the right track.

"Commitments? I want to honor and obey God in everything. And when I fail, to bounce back quickly.

"What's the Lord doing? Seems it's pretty much what I've been saying, and now you believe me. I think He's correcting us and making us His own.

"Strange aspects?

"The delivery person could've been an Angel.

"The color changes? Sky blue is blue sky, meaning Heaven, where the shipments came from. The only thing I can guess is He knows you're not ready yet. Maybe I'm wrong.

"Disappearing instructions? Same thing.

"The food bags teleported back to my car? The people who disrespected God's gift.

"Your absence from both deliveries? Same response as for the disappearing things.

"Your turn, honey."

Bella gave Eddie a tender smile. "Since I totally agree with every word you said, I'll just amplify a few things.

"What's the Lord doing? He's trying to help two of His children and prepare them for the Kingdom. Why He chose us, we may never know this side of eternity. He is also trying to teach people how much He loves all of us. Maybe we should write a book about this, although would anyone believe it? I didn't at first.

"Lifestyles and Commitment? I think I've reached some important conclusions about myself. I have all the trappings of a believer, but my guts aren't in it. For example, I was too slow getting on board that this was the Lord. I should've been with you getting the food and on the street. And finally, I should've been with you about giving God 100%, not 10%. But baby, I'm with you now!

"Ready for that second cup?"

"Let's go, sugar." Eddie nuzzled Bella from behind.

When they got back to the kitchen, they found all the box material there, including the million dollars. Everything was blue again, and the instructions reappeared.

"Turn around, Eddie." She put her hands on her cheeks. "Another identical box just materialized!"

Bella opened it. "Now, everything's blue, not white, but there are no instructions."

The materialized box also contained a hundred packets valued at $10,000 each. Another million dollars!

The money was in two transparent bags. One had 90 packets, the other 10 packets.

THE GIFT THAT KEEPS GIVING
Nancy Roe

Eighty-five-year-old Earl Melvin sat on the granite curved bench facing his late wife's tombstone. Marigold had died forty-five years ago after a brain aneurysm ruptured during her weekly trip to the grocery store.

Earl ate his lunch (a peanut butter and apricot jam sandwich on white bread, no crust, a single-serving bag of Lays, a chocolate chip cookie, and a bottle of water) with Marigold the second and fourth Tuesday of every month. Even when he worked as a high school science teacher (the strict teacher who kids dreaded), he planned his lunch breaks to visit his wife. In forty years, he had only missed two lunch dates. One because of a wicked snowstorm and the second because of a painful kidney stone. Today, leaves formed to offer shade in the upcoming summer months and daffodils popped out for a drink of sunshine.

"Won't be long, my love," Earl said. "Saw the doctor this morning. My aortic valve is not doing so great. He gave me four to six months. Soon we'll be dancing to Perry Como's *Catch a Falling Star.*" He gathered his belongings in his backpack and, with the support of his cane, began the four-block walk home.

Earl lived in the older part of town where one-story bungalows, six to a block (three each on the east and west sides), were built in the 1940s. His house sat in the middle of the east side, the only one with a six-foot tall wooden fence around his back property. He never had kids or any animals to contain in the backyard, he just liked his privacy.

Up ahead, he spotted Emeline Tucker waiting on the sidewalk like she did the second Tuesday of every month. She began this routine when he started using a cane six months ago. At first, he hated the idea. He could walk the last few steps by himself. But then he thought back to his fall on the uneven sidewalk that prompted the cane usage. He had sat on the sidewalk over thirty minutes before a passerby stopped to help him stand and enter his house.

Emeline was the seventeen-year-old next-door neighbor. She and her mother had moved in next door twelve years ago after her father died of a heart attack while harvesting soybeans. They moved to town after they couldn't afford to stay on the family farm. In the early years, Earl often babysat Emeline, and for the past three years, he helped her with her science studies. She was a dedicated student, had several close friends, and was always working, whether it be babysitting, waitressing, mowing lawns, or raking leaves. Earl admired her commitment.

Emeline hooked her arm around Earl and they walked together to his front door. "I aced the chemistry test, but missed one on the calculus test," she said. "My organic chemistry test is tomorrow afternoon, then microbiology on Thursday. Can't believe I graduate in eleven days."

"Have you started packing for Harvard?" Earl asked as he unlocked the door. "Aren't you moving in five weeks?"

Emeline followed Earl into the kitchen. "I'm waiting until after finals. Besides, my mom hasn't found a place for us to live yet. She found one apartment we could afford, but it's forty-five minutes away and only a one bedroom."

"I feel something will come up in the next few days," Earl said as he set his backpack on the kitchen counter.

Emeline sat at the small table and folded the morning newspaper. "My mom needs some positivity. She's freaking me out. Thank goodness for my scholarships and that she got a job at the university's food services. Did you know they serve over 22,000 meals a day? That's crazy!"

Earl took the paper and plopped it in the recycle bin next to the back door. "It's a big campus. Need to feed those smart minds." His breathing became labored, and he sat at the table across from Emeline.

"It's getting warm. You might want to drive to the cemetery on Thursday."

Earl swatted his hand in the air. "The day I can't walk to see Marigold is the day I die," he said in a crusty voice.

Emeline leaned back in the chair. "You know, I've always been at the top of my class. But a hundred and twenty kids are a lot different from thousands of peers."

"And what have I always told you?"

Emeline took a deep breath. "The difference between who you are and who you want to be is what you do."

Earl nodded. "And it has served you well. I'm very proud of all your accomplishments. I wish I'd be around to see what a talented doctor you will become."

Emeline smiled. She stood and pushed in the chair. "I've got to study. See you on Thursday after my last final. We'll celebrate with a trip to Dairy Queen. I'll buy you a pineapple sundae."

❦

Three weeks later, Emeline and her mother sat across the conference table from attorney Tom Hanson.

"Thank you for coming in this morning," Tom said.

"Are we in trouble? Your secretary didn't tell us what this meeting was about," Carla said. She took her daughter's hand and held it tight. "Emeline and I are due to leave town in two weeks."

"No, you aren't in trouble. In fact, I want to apologize for not having this meeting sooner. Earl Melvin's death extended the process."

"Earl? What does he have to do with this meeting?" Emeline asked as she squeezed her mother's hand. Earl was known for being rough around the edges. Had she inadvertently upset him and this was some sort of payback? She thought they were getting along so well.

"Well, Emeline. Earl named you as his beneficiary. He made several purchases and provisions for you and your mother."

"He did what?" Carla shook her head. "Why would he do that?"

"Although you're not blood relatives, he considered you his family," Tom said.

117

"His family?" Emeline voice cracked. "I didn't know he felt that way. I mean, I treated him like a grandfather figure and I knew I'd miss him while at Harvard. But for him to name me as his beneficiary is unbelievable."

Tom opened a brown leather binder. "We will discuss Earl's will, but first you need to read the letter Earl wrote." Tom handed a sealed envelope to Emeline. "He had planned to give it to you on graduation day."

Emeline ran her hand over her name written in Earl's distinctive cursive lettering, then opened the envelope.

"My dearest Emeline. You may not believe this, considering I know the kids in the neighborhood call me a grumpy old man, but you've given me joy over the last twelve years. My health is declining and although I won't be around to see you become an accomplished doctor, I want you to start the next chapter in your life with a solid foundation.

"First, I paid the mortgage on your home."

Emeline shared a stunned look with her mother. "Is this true?" she asked Tom.

"Absolutely. Keep reading."

"If acceptable to you, a buyer has agreed to buy both your property and mine. I will put the proceeds in a trust that you will receive on your twenty-fifth birthday." Emeline put the letter on her lap and turned to her mom. "This would solve so many problems you've been worried about."

Tom interjected. "There are more surprises."

Carla gasped and spread her fingers against her chest. "There's more?"

Emeline continued reading. "I purchased a condo in Cambridge that will be your home while you study and work at Harvard. It has beautiful views of the river and is within walking distance of campus."

"But we have a lease on an apartment," Carla said. "We had to make a hefty deposit."

Tom said, "It's on the list of things to take care of for you. The estate will refund any monies you already paid, plus pay any amount to break the lease. The condo is quite spectacular, with two bedrooms, three bathrooms, two parking spaces, and over twenty-seven hundred square feet. Plus, Earl paid the HOA fees for the next ten years."

"I don't understand," Emeline said as tears ran down her cheek. "How? Why? I'm at a loss for words."

"Keep reading," Tom said.

"I also made arrangements for two new BMW SUVs for you and your mother. I requested a red one for you, Emeline. When you arrive in Cambridge, visit the BMW dealership on Commonwealth Avenue. Finally, upon my death, you will inherit the money in my Merrill Lynch accounts. You and your mother will live without worry.

"My wish to you is that you share your wealth with others that are less fortunate. Do it in secret. Make it mean something to you. I wish the best for you in the future. Love, Earl."

"This is too much. How did Earl pay for this? I didn't think he had much money," Emeline said as she held the letter tight to her chest.

"Five years ago, he won the mega millions lottery. He took the lump sum and made some wise investments."

"He never said a thing," Emeline said. "A few weeks before he died, he was complaining about the price of eggs."

"Earl enjoyed his simple life. He didn't want others in the community to know he was a multi-millionaire. He made several anonymous donations over the years. Like the new auditorium at the high school and the tennis courts at Tyler Park."

"The anonymous donor was Earl?" Emeline said. The grumpy old man had a heart of gold.

Tom nodded. "Once we go over his will and you sign some paperwork, you'll be the recipient of twelve million dollars."

⁊

Dr. Emeline Tucker crossed the stage and stopped at the podium to address the newest graduates of West Delaware High

School. "After I graduated from this high school, a man I admired gave me a generous gift that I have never mentioned before today. Because of that gift, I started a scholarship fund for future graduates of West Delaware. Four graduates each year have received a $25,000 Earl Melvin Scholarship for their collegiate studies. This year, on the tenth anniversary of Earl's death, I am giving each graduate $10,000 to further their education."

The gymnasium broke into cheers and tears. It took almost ten minutes for the audience to regain their composure.

"There's more. Each graduate will also receive $5,000 to pay forward to fellow college students. While I was at Harvard, I didn't want anyone to know I came into a large sum of money, but I wanted to spread my good fortune to others. In order for my identity to stay secretive, I enrolled the help of my counselor to hand out what I called 'my happy gifts.' These gifts varied from Starbucks gift cards, gift cards to the local bookstore, or a simple 'You are Wonderful' card with a hundred-dollar bill.

"My wish for you is that you follow my lead. Be the secret of goodwill toward your peers. Not only will the recipient of your gift be blessed, but so will you."

Emeline sat on the curved granite bench and gave Earl an overview of the past ten years. She told him stories of her college professors, study groups, and her charity work for the heart association. "Tomorrow I'm hosting the first 'Earl Melvin 5K Run' to support the science department at the high school. We have over a hundred runners signed up for the event. There's going to be food trucks, games, and prizes."

Emeline stood and laid a bouquet of red roses on the grave. "And just between you and me, an anonymous donor will make a donation at the last minute to bring the total raised to $100,000. Rest in peace, Earl, and thank you for my astonishing life."

Editor's note: In gaming and hacking jargon, "pwn" means to overtake, to possess by force. It's pronounced "pone".

PWN WAR: X5 HUSTLE
Wallace M. Graham

MC Lars blasted through the speakers of Asher's new BMW X5. He adjusted the rearview mirror, aimed at his backpack in the back seat behind him. While checking his hair and teeth, he turned into Harper's driveway. After honking the horn several times, he unbuckled his seat belt, popped open the door, and bounced out of the vehicle in a near simultaneous motion. He strutted to its front and bounced on the balls of his feet for a second or two. His bouncing, after a second, combined with pacing. He froze in place and locked his eyes upon Harper's front door when it opened.

Harper burst out the front door and stopped halfway down the walkway. She gasped and covered her mouth. Her wide eyes studied the 2024 BMW X5 Mid-size Sport Utility Vehicle (SUV). Its metallic gray-green color shimmered in the afternoon sun as it rumbled from the low bass beats playing within it.

"Omigosh! Is this why you skipped school?"

"What do you think?" he asked, splaying his arms at the SUV.

"How did you pay for it?"

"Bitcoin," he said, raising on his toes and pulling on the zippered centerlines of his maroon Collierville Dragons hoodie. "You're looking at the first high school millionaire in Collierville."

Harper raised an eyebrow and delivered an incredulous smile.

"A lucky investment windfall…I swear," he said. He waggled his eyebrows and beamed a teeth-filled grin. "You wanna drive?"

She pranced past him in a blur and opened the driver side door. "Get in."

He snickered and stuffed his hands into the pockets of his hoodie. With a pivot, he turned to the passenger door. Sliding into the seat and shutting the door, he tapped the screen of his cradle-mounted smart phone and changed the playlist.

Harper giggled as Taylor Swift's voice filled the cabin. She buckled her seatbelt while dancing to the music. Adjusting the seat and checking the mirrors, she grabbed and yanked back on the gearshift.

"Whoa!" Asher yelled over the music. He poked the power button. "You can't do that. It's an electric gearshift."

"I didn't know. Sorry!" she yelled back.

Asher closed his eyes and exhaled. "It's okay. You probably didn't break it." He wiggled the gearshift several times to be sure. "Look. It's connected to the SUV's computer. You only need to nudge it." He demonstrated by nudging the gearshift into reverse and back into park. Raising his eyes, he angled his head to make confirmation with her eyes. She frowned and averted her eyes.

"So, where we going?" he asked in a playful tone.

She met his gaze and curled her lips into a slight smile. Then, she flashed him an impish grin. "Let's get Leslie. We can wait in the parking lot until she's done cheerleading. She'll flip when she sees your new car."

"The wheel is yours," he said and turned on the music. He leaned back and buckled his seatbelt.

With a giggle, she bounced in her seat several times and made a deliberate show of nudging the SUV into reverse. She backed out of the driveway and headed to Byhalia Road. At Byhailia, she turned and went south while Asher and she sang along to her favorite song. At the red light in front of the West Collierville Middle School, her singing degraded into laughter because Asher butchered the lyrics.

"You're terrible," she said between laughs. He continued for a few more words until the engine revved.

"Okay, no need to protest," he said with raised hands. "I'll stop."

"That wasn't me," she said while shaking her head in small movements.

The SUV rolled forward into the intersection. Harper gasped. Asher bounced his gaze around the dashboard.

"Smash the brake!" he said.

"I am! It's not working!"

He grabbed and flipped the gearshift. It remained in drive.

Harper unbuckled her seatbelt. She yanked on the door handle, but the autolock feature countered. Asher mashed the switches on the armrest to open the window or stop the autolock action. The SUV lurched forward with acceleration. Harper yelped and grasped the steering wheel with both hands. It fought her grip and turned on its own. Climbing to eighty miles per hour, it passed several vehicles weaving between the lanes of traffic. It closed in on the Powell Road intersection.

Harper screamed with hysterical sobs. She smacked the steering wheel and stomped at the pedals. Asher braced himself against his seat, mounting his arms against the door and center console. The approaching stoplight changed from green to yellow.

He looked at the dashboard, Harper's panic, and the center console area. His eyes flashed wide and snagged the emergency brake. Yanking it, the cabin filled with the smell of burnt brake pads as the vehicle lost speed. Then, it stopped, fifty feet from the intersection. He exhaled and relaxed into his seat. Harper whimpered and trembled in her seat.

"Where my money?" a Russian sounding male voice asked over the SUV's stereo system.

"Wh-What? Who are you?" Asher asked, staring at his phone.

"This not punXworX? Asher—"

"Let me out," Harper shrilled. "Let me out," she repeated through her sobs.

"What? You on date with pretty girl, vor?" he asked and chuckled. "Not go well?"

Asher and Harper looked at each other. Her tear-ridden expression twisted into a wild scowl. "You stole from Russians? What's wrong with you?"

"They're lying! I didn't steal anything."

"Nyet, enough game. We know it's you," the voice said. "We trace bitcoin. You never tumble. Make easy to find."

Other vehicles stacked behind the SUV and honked. Some pulled around and passed on the driver's side. Harper banged on the window and yelled for help. The passing drivers either scowled or gave quizzical looks.

"Give back my money, vor," the voice blared through the speakers at max volume. Asher cringed in his seat covering his ears. Harper screamed while covering her ears.

"I don't have it," Asher said.

The voice growled. It calmed and said, "I like fancy car, everything electronic."

Asher held his breath. Harper made quiet whimpers. They turned their heads toward each other and stared. A metal click broke the silence. Harper's face transformed into an expression of hysteria. The vehicle rolled forward.

"We pwn fancy car. We pwn you. You pay one way or other," the voice said.

Taylor Swift boomed through the speakers. The SUV darted through the intersection and swiped a Ford F150 truck. Harper shrilled, clutching the steering wheel. Asher covered his face and head with his arms upon impact. After, he craned his head to see the F150 skid to a stop.

The SUV gained speed. Drowned by the music, Asher recognized Harper screaming at him. "I hate you," and "You did this," penetrated the music clearer than the rest of her words. He clenched his grip upon the console and tightened his jaw. With a huff, he yanked his phone from its cradle and threw it into the back seat behind Harper. She flinched, and the music stopped.

"They're supposed to be anonymous. This never happens." His voice rose with hysteria. "No one does this."

"I hate you," she yelled, emphasizing each word at the top of her lungs.

The SUV bounced off a vehicle and jumped the median into oncoming traffic. It blitzed through the White Road intersection. Clipping a Chevrolet Silverado, it swerved back into ongoing traffic and bounced off another car. The sounds of skidding tires squealed behind them and ended with the smashing of metal. Traffic increased around them as they encroached upon one of the busiest intersections in Collierville: Poplar Avenue.

"Ready to pay?" the voice resounded in the cabin.

"Let me go," Harper said in repetition as she sobbed.

Asher stared at the console with a blank mystified expression. Then, he darted his gaze behind Harper's seat. The sight of his bobbing backpack stirred him into action.

"Answer, vor," the voice boomed through the speakers.

Asher ignored the voice. He extended his body and reached into the backseat. The seatbelt dug into his neck. Harper panicked and rained blows upon his head and right forearm which shielded him. His fingers flicked at the backpack's grab handle as claw marks oozed blood from his face. The SUV swerved and clipped another car. The motion pitched Asher into his seat against the door. He smiled at the sight of his backpack perched on the console with its grab handle still in hand.

"I know you hear," the voice said. "Give me my money."

Asher unzipped his backpack and pulled his laptop. He reached in it again and pulled various cables. Opening the glovebox, he grabbed the owner's manual and tossed it into the backseat. He reached into the glovebox and searched. Harper's scream followed by an impact and scraping of metal distracted him. He latched onto his computer before it dropped. He reached into the glovebox again and found the USB port to the SUV's computer.

Connecting his computer via a cable, he searched for the main operating system of the SUV computer. Clicking through the admin settings, he took control of the SUV. The vehicle's speed dropped. He proceeded without stopping at his keyboard. His eyes raced across the screen. With a few strokes, he disabled the stereo system.

"I want—" the Russian voice dropped before finishing.

Harper perked up when she noticed the speed drop. She glanced through each window. Stopping on Asher, she asked, "You're hacking the car?"

"If they can do it, so can I," Asher said, not looking at her.

However, the SUV did not slow fast enough. It barreled straight toward the rear end of a Chevrolet Tahoe stopped at the Academy Sports+Outdoors intersection.

Harper mashed the brakes. "Stop," she yelled into the steering wheel. "You stupid car. Stop."

Asher found the controls for the steering wheel and brakes. Looking up from his computer, he tapped several keys. The SUV swerved and skidded past the Tahoe. It jumped the curb and slowed to a stop inside the Academy parking lot. He killed the engine and closed his laptop. He looked at Harper.

She trembled in her seat and scanned through each window. Meeting his gaze, she said, "Stay away from me." The sound of Collierville police cars racing toward them caught her attention. After a ragged sigh, she popped the door and ran towards them.

Asher watched as one cop wrapped his arms around her and followed her accusatory finger in his direction. Out of nowhere, Asher's passenger door flew open. A hand grabbed the collar of his hoodie while an arm wrapped around his head in a choke hold. He lost his computer as another set of hands smacked it away and cut his seatbelt.

Yanking him out of the SUV, two cops pinned him to the pavement. They twisted his arms behind him and slapped on a set of handcuffs. Pulling him to his feet, one read him his rights while the other dragged him to the police car and stuffed him into it. They met with the other set of officers by Harper.

Asher waited and listened to the police radio. He watched as an FBI agent arrived and talked to Harper. A team of law enforcement collected his computer and searched the SUV.

One mistake. I lost it all because of one mistake, he thought. He snorted and broke a small smile. *At least, I'm a minor. Maybe they'll go easy since this is my first offense?*

The driver door opened and one of the cops entered. He closed the door and adjusted in his seat to see Asher.

"Hey, is that girl for real? You stole a million dollars from Russians?" he asked.

Asher smiled and nodded.

"Don't smile. You know you're in trouble, right? That's the FBI talking to your girl."

His smile fell and his eyes stared into the protective barrier.

"She's not my girl. The Russians ruined that."

Before the police officer continued, static and squelch burst from the radio. A voice broke through the static.

"This car with Asher, Mr. Policeman?" the Russian voice asked.

"What the—? Who's this?" the officer asked into the microphone.

"I wish to send message."

"I don't have it," Asher said. The officer repeated his words into the radio.

The voice laughed. "You lucky. Police car not hack, so I pwn radio."

Asher saw the FBI agent and law enforcement team scramble outside. The agent ran toward their car.

"This not over. You run like little baby," the voice said. "We will find you. I will get my money."

The radio silenced and returned to its normal status. The police officer turned to look at Asher again. "Boy, what did you start?"

Asher shrugged as a tear dropped from his face onto hands. In a soft voice, he answered, "Pwn War."

AUTHOR BIOS

STEVE BRADSHAW, Forensic Investigator, Biotech Entrepreneur, Darrel Award Mystery/Thriller author and Ghostwriter with 10 novels (softcover/eBooks) and 5 audiobooks (Amazon Audible) available worldwide, and 1 screenplay TERMINAL BREACH. Steve is currently writing Book II of The Hillsborough Trilogy for release Fall 2022, and a new novella series John Ritzinger—PI for release in the Spring 2023. www.stevebradshawauthor.com

JOHN BURGETTE writes in several styles, including poetry, research, sermons, and short stories. His background includes computer science, social sciences, academic research, and lay ministry. Besides contributing to several of the CC Writers' anthologies, his creative writing has appeared in *Southern Writers Magazine* and *Tennessee Magazine*.

KAREN BUSLER is a professional symphony orchestra musician (retired), writer, choir director, Bible study leader, and amateur chef. She has been a finalist and third place winner in *Southern Writers Magazine* Short Story competitions. Her full life includes writing, swimming, singing, studying, hosting parties, or making her award-winning chili! Contact her at www.karenbusler.com.

BETH KREWSON CARTER received her degree from Meredith College, then went to work for Procter & Gamble. Later, while raising a family, she taught school for several years. She studied creative writing with Laura Grabowski-Cotton and has written for *Woman's World* magazine. She currently lives in Tennessee with her husband and the youngest of their three children. *Poison Root* is her second novel, *The Nest Keeper* was her debut in 2019.

JUDY CREEKMORE wrote for the *Times-Picayune* for 25 years. She published *Celebrating 200 Years of River Parishes History* in 2008 and has penned two unpublished cozy mysteries. Her short fiction has appeared in various anthologies. She encourages others to write by word and example.

FRANK DiBIANCA devotes his retirement years to writing suspense novels, like *Laser Trap* (A Quincy U Suspense*)*, containing an award-winning sauce of romance, mystery, and action on a bed of faith. His employers included the Fermi National Accelerator Laboratory, General Electric Medical Systems, U North Carolina – Chapel Hill, and U Tennessee Health Science Center. Frank was the principal designer of the General Electric 9800 CT Scanner.

KAY DIBIANCA is a former software developer and IT manager who retired to a life of mystery. She's the award-winning author of the Watch Series of cozy mysteries. Kay and her husband, Frank, live and write in Memphis, TN. Connect with Kay on her website at https://kaydibianca.com.

GARY FEARON is a writer, producer and musician. He has written over 300 songs, advertising jingles and morning show parodies. His published works include short stories and the books *After Abbey Road: The Solo Hits of The Beatles* and *Right Brain Writing: Creative Shortcuts for Wordsmiths*. Visit him at www.garyfearon.com.

LARRY FITZGERALD is a retired businessman who enjoys writing Christian fiction, including romance and mystery. He is a former youth soccer coach and feels it is important to encourage Christian worldview thinking in the hearts and minds of our young adults.

WALLACE M. GRAHAM sharpened his pencil by achieving a master's in criminology. Living in Toone, Tennessee, he develops his craft through experiences at the Collierville Christian Writers Club, the Word Weavers of West Tennessee, and multiple edits of unpublished works through Writer's Digest. Through the writing club, he self-published short stories, annually, as part of an anthology. Other official writings fall into the academic areas of interest.

RONALD LLOYD: Over the years, I found myself rewriting plots in my head or jotting down an outline on scraps of paper. At sixty-six I retired to a back booth of a Burger King and began writing. Hope you enjoy what I created as much as I have enjoyed writing it.

ANNETTE COLE MASTRON started her writing career in the insurance industry working for over 35 years as an investigator, writing reports for a variety of clients. In 2012, she changed careers to work as Communications Director for *Southern Writers Magazine* and its blog, Suite T. She wrote for both the magazine and blog until it closed. A charter member of CCWriters, she is contributing author to twelve anthology books and is writing her first book. She is Editor-in-Chief of this anthology.

NICK NIXON is a published author, illustrator and audiobook narrator of five Peter English, PI novels and six children's books. He also writes articles and cartoons for various publications. He is currently writing a western and another detective novel. And he does illustrations and audiobook narrations for other authors.

DOYNE PHILLIPS is the Co-founder, Charter Member, and past Vice President of Collierville Christian Writers. He has contributed short stories to ten of CCWriters' eleven anthologies. He was also Co-founder and Managing Editor of *Southern Writers Magazine*, where he wrote numerous articles and over 230 blogs for their online site.

BARBARA RAGSDALE is an award-winning writer in short stories. She is published in three Chicken Soup for the Soul anthologies and multiple short-story collections published by CC Writers. Her story "A Walking Miracle" is published in Guideposts' *Miracles Do Happen*. Her poem "Final Moments" will be published in *Can,Sir! Moments*. She was a columnist and staff writer for *Southern Writers Magazine*. When not writing, she is an exercise instructor with the Silver Sneakers program.

NANCY ROE has self-published eight books. *The Accident* won the Gold Quill Award, and *Butterfly Premonitions* won First Place for the first chapter. Nancy is a member of Sisters in Crime, The League of Utah Writers, and Newsletter Chair of the Newcomers Club of the Greater Park City Area.

JAN WERTZ is enjoying retirement life by turning her imagination loose as a writer, photographer, and traveler. One of her travel addictions is to sign on as a tourist with a storm chasing expert and his tour guides. A DAR, her writing frequently includes her family memoirs.

Also by C C WRITERS

www.ingramcontent.com/pod-product-compliance
Lightning Source LLC
Chambersburg PA
CBHW071154300726
48975CB00004B/1155